THE HEIR OF FRINTON PARK

THE HEIR OF FRINTON PARK

Freda M. Long

Chivers Press • G.K. Hall & Co
Bath, England   Thorndike, Maine USA

This Large Print edition is published by Chivers Press, England, and by G.K. Hall & Co., USA.

Published in 1998 in the U.K. by arrangement with Robert Hale Ltd.

Published in 1998 in the U.S. by arrangement with Robert Hale Ltd.

U.K. Hardcover ISBN 0–7540–3131–4 (Chivers Large Print)
U.K. Softcover ISBN 0–7540–3132–2 (Camden Large Print)
U.S. Softcover ISBN 0–7838–8290–4 (Nightingale Collection Edition)

The text of this Large Print edition is unabridged.
Other aspects of the book may vary from the original edition.

Set in 16 pt. New Times Roman.

Printed in Great Britain on acid-free paper.

British Library Cataloguing in Publication Data available

Library of Congress Cataloging-in-Publication Data

Long, Freda Margaret.
  The heir of Frinton Park / Freda M. Long.
    p. cm.
  ISBN 0–7838–8290–4 (large print : sc : alk. paper)
  1. Large type books. I. Title.
[PR6062.O512H4   1998]
823′.914—dc21
                                                        97–30902

MARCH/APRIL, 1790

James Darker receives an interesting proposition

It was now three months since James Darker had followed the body of his mother across the park to the family mausoleum and had listened, with complete indifference, to Parson Ellsworthy intoning the words of the burial service in his customary nasal chant. 'Man that is born of woman hath but a short time to live and is full of misery. He cometh up, and is cut down like a flower...'

At the time of her death, from a congestion of the lungs, Clarissa Darker had just passed her forty-first birthday. In an age when the average life-span of a human being was statistically placed at forty-seven she could not be said to have fared too badly, though it did seem a thought unfair that her mother, old Lady Elizabeth Branson, should still be wheezily breathing the air of this world and quaffing her nightly glass of smuggled brandy with undiminished relish.

The forces, unseen and omnipotent, which determine the destiny of each individual upon this earth take delight in dispensing the gifts at their disposal with devilish partiality. This and a heterogeneous collection of other, less

1

relevant thoughts, passed through the head of James Darker as the doleful ceremony proceeded, and he marvelled at the callous dryness of his own eyes when everyone about him was busily collecting memorial tears in the tiny glass receptacles thoughtfully provided for the mourners by Messrs. Weller and Thompson, the Brighthelmstone undertakers.

Only James's favourite sister Amelia, thankfully concealing the strawberry birthmark upon her left cheek behind three layers of black gauze, understood what prompted her brother's seemingly unnatural behaviour. Amelia knew that all his grief for his dearest Mama, so admirably contained, would be poured forth behind the dusty curtains of his bed, or perhaps in the enveloping blackness of the linen closet, the latter a place where all the Darker children had assuaged with tears the stinging rebukes and blows meted out by their elders and betters.

Aunts, uncles, sisters, cousins and servants, all bearing the appearance of black, bedraggled crows, trooped back to the house across the springy turf of the magnificent lawns, each one looking forward eagerly to the dispensation of Mr. William Darker's fine Madeira as a necessary restorative to flagging spirits. James parted company from them at the foot of the elegant staircase which curved upwards from the chequered floor of the hall, and having negotiated the polished oaken treads in three or four athletic bounds, barged like a blinded bull through the door of his chamber, there to weep until he should be summoned to supper.

Such is the nature of man, however, that within a month of the foregoing sad event the resilience of youth had more or less reasserted itself, and James emerged from his period of mourning to contemplate his prospects for the future. The anarchic conditions under which he had studied Latin and Greek at his public school at Winchester, and where he had once been bullied into making twelve pieces of toast with his bare hands almost touching the red-hot coals, had done little to fit him for a future career.

Three years at Oxford as a Gentleman Commoner had taught him nothing more significant than how to hold his liquor and to converse pleasantly when endowed with the signal honour of dining at the Dons' High Table. He was therefore left with the sobering conclusion that there were only two alternatives open to him. He could enter the confused world of politics, handing out *douceurs* to the Mayor and Corporation of Brighthelmstone and relying upon the Earl of Adur, his father's friend, to bludgeon the electors into voting for him, or, like his father, he could become a dealer in human flesh. He found the former prospect more appealing, sharing his late mother's views that the buying and selling of black-skinned men, women and children was a thoroughly disagreeable proceeding.

James had always been careful never to debate the rights and wrongs of slave-trafficking with his father, while discussing them at length with his mother. That sweet soul had never betrayed him, though she must sometimes have longed publicly to proclaim an ally in her lengthy and unsuccessful bid to turn her husband from the error of his ways. Of Clarissa's five daughters only poor, afflicted Amelia, with her strawberry mark and one leg slightly shorter than the other, had fought the good fight, reading aloud from the London sheets the expressions of Mr. William Wilberforce's disgust as he thundered forth anathema against the vile abuses practised upon the dignity of 'our black brethren.' William Darker had long since ceased to be irritated by these blatant and ostentatious attempts to appeal to the better side of his nature. Amusement had superseded initial displeasure, for he had his womenfolk firmly under control and could afford to view their little foibles with an indulgent eye.

Whichever way he chose to go—and it had not escaped James's notice that ultimately his father might make the choice for him—one thing was certain, he was honour-bound to marry Miss Mary Houghton, the heiress from Steynford, whose father had baited the trap

4

with a marriage settlement of £150,000. It was an enormous price to pay for one's only daughter to marry the son of a simple gentleman, but then Mary Houghton was enormously plain, with nothing to commend her save the fact that she had never been known to express an opinion and seemed to regard herself as a natural slave to the male of the species. James had already resigned himself to the fact that he would have to look elsewhere if the thrills and ecstasies of sexual union were not to elude him, but he thought this no bad thing, since he conformed to the general opinion prevailing among gentlemen of the period that wives were provided by God for the begetting of children and mistresses for the exercise of delight.

William Darker had looked upon the capture of Miss Houghton as singularly fortunate, for the Abolitionists, after pot-shotting at the slave-dealers for upwards of twenty years, were now firmly entrenched in the hallowed halls of Westminster, and with the redoubtable Mr. Wilberforce at their head would sooner or later declare themselves the victors as they watched their Bill to abolish the slave-trade pass from Commons to Lords. £150,000 was a nice little guarantee against the insecurity of the future. Come the day when four unseaworthy slavers found their way to the breaker's yard, repinings at the loss of a profitable business venture would be somewhat alleviated by the thought of Mary Houghton's dowry.

One morning in mid-April James's musings upon his future were cut short by a request from his father that he would please to present himself in the library 'immediately upon the stroke of ten'. The young man obeyed the summons with a sinking heart, convinced that the subject matter of the coming interview between himself and his father was related to one of two things. Either an announcement concerning his official betrothal to Miss Houghton was to be made, or Mr. Darker had found out about his son's nightly fumblings with little Susannah in the linen-closet. The latter seemed the more likely contingency since his mother had been dead less than four months and the required period of mourning, during which announcements of betrothals were taboo, was one year.

William Darker strongly disapproved of love intrigues taking place under his roof. Twenty years ago there had occurred a horrifying episode concerning a distant female cousin and William Darker's own brother, the details of which were known only to the older members of the family. Since that time any burgeoning relationships between male members of the family and female servants or lowly dependents had been firmly nipped in the bud. Even old Uncle Richard, scandalously divorced and disreputable, retired from the army on an insufficient pension and heavily dependent on his elder brother's patrimony, had been reprimanded like a schoolboy for squeezing between thumb and forefinger the cook's temptingly ample posterior.

The first thing that met James's eye as he entered the library was the portrait of his mother, painted by Sir Joshua Reynolds, which hung over the Adam-style fireplace. It was what people quaintly referred to as a 'speaking likeness'. As a child James had often stood before the portrait, looking up at the gently smiling lips, and fancying that they formed a word especially for him. The word might be 'sweetheart', or 'precious', or simply 'Jemmy', always something to reflect the way he felt about her and the way she felt about him. It was a fascinating game which he did not outgrow until he went up to Oxford. His first half at that unholy establishment successfully eradicated the boyish sentimentality of his early years, and replaced it with the diamond-hard attitude of the young virile male. Fortunately, not even Oxford could brutalise a youth whose goodness of heart was continually proclaimed through his consideration for others, and after he quitted the esteemed and ancient pile of King's he quickly mellowed. The more mature James was content merely to gaze upon the well-loved face of his mother and be glad that the great artist had preserved those pleasant lineaments with such accuracy for the constant delight of her family. Blonde and grey-eyed, Clarissa Darker stared serenely back at her loved ones, intelligently amused by their antics.

William Darker sat entrenched behind his large mahogany desk, which bravely bore the weight of several leather-bound tomes, a score of unfinished letters, two large pewter ink-pots and a forest of broken quill pens. He looked up as his son entered and pushed aside the letter he had been perusing, which carried the flamboyant signature of his friend and business associate, Charles Oliver, Earl of Adur. The letter, engraved with the Earl's family crest and a facsimile of his country seat at Penworth, bore unmistakable signs of having been frequently handled.

William inserted an inquiring finger under his Cadogan wig and scratched his balding head. His stone-blue, slightly bloodshot eyes, peered out above the plump scarlet mounds of his cheeks, and his large front teeth chewed absently on his bottom lip. 'How would you like to make the Grand Tour?'

The question, flung at him like a challenge, took James completely by surprise. Thoughts of Susannah, wriggling against him in the linen-closet, faded, as he struggled to accept this new, quite unexpected proposition.

William's forefinger stabbed at the much thumbed letter. 'I could not afford such high-falutin' nonsense myself, you understand, but

Adur is determined that his youngest son, Lord Frederick, shall make the Tour, and he has asked me if I will give my consent to your accompanying Lord Frederick and his tutor. He has offered to pay all your expenses.'

'Why?'

William made a sound between a laugh and a grunt. 'You may well ask. His lordship thinks,'—and here the letter was snatched up and impatiently consulted— ' "that young James, being of a sober and upright disposition, will have a salutary effect upon the wilder traits of my son's character"—'how's that for self-deception?'

James met his father eye to eye and unwittingly caused a swift pang of grief to catch the older man unawares. Those grey eyes, so like Clarissa's, out-staring the world, prepared to defend to the death every foolish and high ideal, whatever the strength of the enemy who misguidedly opposed; that same pale complexion and firm yet gentle mouth; that same slightly arrogant nose; that same hair, light as corn, curling about his ears and forehead; that same stubborn conviction that he was *right*.

With Clarissa William had always used attack as the best means of defence, and so it was with her son, *her* son because he could see so little of William Darker in James. He said, 'Do not think for one moment that a spell on the Continent will let you off marrying Miss

9

Houghton. It will only be for a year at the most and she can wait that long. I doubt she will even notice you've gone, you pay so little attention to her.'

'That is because I do not love her,' James returned coolly, but with the challenge there in his voice, ready for William to pick up. On this occasion his father chose to ignore it, though the sound of Clarissa's voice, echoing down the years, came back to him with a clarity so astonishingly fresh that her words might have been spoken yesterday. 'I should so much like it if you were to love me for myself, William, and not just because I am to bear your child.'

Abruptly he dismissed the ghostly presence, riposting harshly, 'Try lavishing your affections on £150,000. That should fetch the colour to your cheeks, and in case you are wondering what I meant by his lordship deceiving himself, I refer to your nightly fornications with Susannah in the linen-closet, brought to my notice by a series of grunts and groans overheard by the skivvy, who fled shrieking down to Cook to report the presence of a ghost in the house. Word soon got around, and the tale fetched up in my ear. It did not take me long to trace the 'haunting' to its source, and you may be gratified to know that since I thought it high time you lost your virginity I allowed your little trysts to proceed undisturbed for a while. I take it you've got the hang of it by now?'

10

To his annoyance James felt himself blushing. He muttered, 'I had to start somewhere.'

'But not in your own backyard,' returned his father testily. 'Why did you not tell *me* that you needed a woman? I'd have fixed you up with one of your Aunt Sophie's maids.'

'Papa!' protested James, the colour in his cheeks deepening, 'I have been in need of a woman, as you so quaintly describe it, for at least four years, ever since my sixteenth birthday in fact. It is only by a miracle of self-control that I have managed to curb my natural instincts until recently. Papa, I am twenty!'

'Yes, I find that hard to believe,' growled William, pushing back his chair and hefting his ponderous bulk to the perpendicular. 'Can it really be true that three years at Oxford did not rob you of your virginity?' He came round to the front of the desk, bending upon his son a look in which frank amusement warred with outright derision.

James turned to face him and confessed, 'I was fearful of catching a dose. The Duke of Bedford's youngest son William used to make jests about taking so many mercury pills that he had turned into a human barometer.'

William's eyebrows rose. 'You young men are getting careless. In my day we used to pay an apothecary to examine the girls before we took them to bed.'

'A thought cold-blooded,' commented James.

'And safe!' snapped William. 'But we are digressing.' He spread his hands over his full-blown paunch, his finger-tips enjoying the feel of rich ribbed satin. 'His lordship desires that the tour shall commence at the beginning of May, so you've just a couple of weeks in which to make your preparations. I have a list somewhere which his lordship enclosed with his letter ... deuce take it, where the devil ...?' He leant over the desk, irritably shuffling his papers into further confusion.

'Is this it?' James picked up a sheet of foolscap paper, covered in the neat copperplate of the Earl's secretary. William pounced on it gratefully. 'Ah, so 'tis.' He scanned it carefully. 'I must say, it is a mighty long list. You had better get your sisters to help you with it. They've an enthusiasm for shopping which amounts to a mania.'

Still perusing the list he read out, ' "Lice-proof, taffeta-lined waistcoats—two." Odd's fish, Jemmy, but ye're taking your life in your hands ... which reminds me, his lordship says that you are on no account to stay above a month in Paris. When commoners start dictating to kings there's no knowing what may come of it.'

His son's wide-eyed, faintly apprehensive regard prompted William to add, 'It is safe enough at the moment, provided you do not poke your nose into anything that does not concern you, and you are not likely to do that with the worthy Mr. Brookes at your heels.' The Reverend Arthur Brookes was Lord Frederick's tutor.

'If the situation in France gets out of hand, will it mean war?' asked James.

William shrugged. 'Perhaps, but they've not gone far enough yet.'

James looked at him curiously. 'What more can they do?'

'A devil of a lot,' came the grim reply. 'Last year they stormed the Bastille and committed some particularly nasty atrocities on innocent people. If they organise themselves properly they can depose the King and Queen and set up a Republic in place of the monarchy, a coup which would cause certain highly-placed persons on this side of the Channel to shake in their boots, I can tell you. Here,'—he thrust the list of 'Requirements for Travel Abroad' at James. 'Forget politics for the moment and deal with this. You've not much time.'

James took the list. Little waves of anticipation began to churn up his stomach. 'I shall see all the paintings in the Louvre ... and the Parthenon at Rome ... and the ruins of Pompeii...'

William raised a sardonic eyebrow. 'Aye, and a few more things you won't bargain for I shouldn't wonder. Get along now, Jemmy. I've a letter to write to my agents in London about a replacement for Captain Gomez on "The Arethusa." He has served me well, but he is getting too old for the job, and 'tis time I pensioned him off.'

On his way downstairs James encountered Susannah struggling upwards with a mound of clean linen in her arms. He followed her into the linen-closet.

APRIL, 1790

Introducing Lord Frederick Oliver

Towards the end of April, with winter still in full cry and masquerading as spring, and the yellow Lenten lilies giving the lie to the cold wind and icy rain-storms, Lord Frederick Oliver came to Frinton Park to visit his would-be fellow-traveller. Arriving in a battered gig of extraordinary antiquity, the only conveyance which his father would permit him to remove from the Penworth stables, this tall, incredibly thin and excessively lively young gentleman drove his vehicle at breakneck speed up the drive of the park, eliciting volleys of oaths from the under-gardener, and pulled up at the front door with a savage crunching of wheels and a frantic jingling of harness as the mare angrily tossed her head in violent protest at this unseemly

14

behaviour. The gentle hands of two stable-boys quickly calmed her down, and she was led decorously away to recover her lost dignity.

Fred took the steps leading to the front door in two energetic bounds and ran full-tilt into the Misses Amelia, Augusta and Sarah Darker, who, complete with furred pelisses and silk parasols, were emerging from the house to take the air. Augusta and Sarah, aged eighteen and seventeen respectively, smiled prettily at Fred, shook their fair curls and teased him with two pairs of identical blue eyes. Their elder sister Amelia, the sad marring of whose features denied her the luxury of coquetry, murmured a quiet, 'Good-afternoon, Lord Frederick,' and would have brushed past him had not Fred seized her gloved hand in order to press it to his lips.

Hazel eyes stared into blue. 'Your hat, Miss Amelia, is distractingly fetching, and far superior to anything worn by the ladies at Ascot this year.'

A quick blush dyed Amelia's cheeks, and she turned her head in the instinctive and habitual gesture of one who always has something to hide. The anguish in her eyes was so potent that Fred was filled with the urgent desire to reach out and pluck it away. Did she distrust every compliment paid to her as having been inspired solely by pity? She seemed unable to recognise a fellow's admiration for her other, less obvious qualities; her haste to make amends

15

when one's feelings were hurt by a careless or cruel word; her compassion for those in trouble; her refusal to speak ill of another. Fred was still too immature to convey such notions to the wilting Amelia. A sentence could have made her the happiest creature alive. Alas, it was not forthcoming.

With a courteous bow and the sweeping off of his tall beaver hat Lord Frederick disappeared into the house, and the young ladies, sighing briefly at having to dispense with the company of the only unattached young gentleman who had visited the house for a month, went off to begin their walk to the village.

Fred waved aside an inquiring footman, who caught his hat, gloves and cane with amazing dexterity, and directed his feet towards the Music Room, which was situated at the front of the house. Sounds of a *Viola d'Amore* in torment told him that his guess was correct. Taking the precaution of placing both hands over his ears, he proceeded on tip-toe and peered round the half-opened door. The sight that met his eyes was impressive, for during the years in which William Darker had been the owner of Frinton Park the Music Room had become the showpiece of the house, superseding the upstairs salon as a place for formal entertainments on a small scale. Large silvered mirrors gave an impression of immense length and breadth to the room, and a minstrel's gallery effect had been produced by the placing of simulated pillars in front of a decorated alcove. Chandeliers of twisted ormolu were reflected in each of the huge mirrors, and the fireplace of Italian marble depicted Aesop's fable of the fox and the stork. The whole had been a happy inspiration of Clarissa's, and represented in its splendour one of the rare occasions on which her advice had been heeded by William.

James, struggling with a part of Mr. Handel's 'Rinaldo', remained oblivious to critical observation until after a series of chromatic scales had completely floored him, whereupon he flung the beautiful instrument aside with an exclamation of disgust and made for the door. Fred's disembodied face cracked into a grin. 'Fan me, Jemmy, but I thought you were torturing Gussie's cat!'

James whirled round with a smile upon his face as broad as a river. 'Fred, my dear fellow, do come in! You have rescued me from an afternoon of incredible boredom. Caroline and Elizabeth are with their governess, Father has gone into Lewes, and the other three girls are just this moment gone down to Piddingfold village to pick up my box of medicines from the apothecary. According to your esteemed Papa, foreign physicians are not to be trusted.'

Fred stepped into the Music Room. 'For your information, my dear James, Papa don't trust foreign cooks either. Fact is, he don't trust anything that ain't true British.'

James laughed. 'Did his lordship make the Grand Tour?'

By this time Fred was preening himself in front of one of the mirrors, admiring the cut of his bottle-green frock-coat and his fawn pantaloons. 'Never heard him talk of it,' he answered carelessly. 'He was probably too busy paying court to his first wife.'

'I hope my father does not marry again,' James said abruptly.

Fred tore himself away from the contemplation of his fashionable attire to stare at his friend. 'Why on earth not? It's the usual thing, you know, if a gentleman don't want to stay celibate, or play around with whores.' He added with his gently teasing smile, 'There stands before you at this very moment the ripening fruit of a second union. Wouldn't you like a little brother who will one day be a comfort to you in your old age, as I am to Charlie and Johnnie?'

A suspicion of brightness lurked in James's eye. 'Mama ...' he began awkwardly. 'Deuce take it, Fred, no one *could* take Mama's place.' Tears, which he was not ashamed to shed before his friend, ran down his cheeks. He dabbed at them with his wrist-band, murmuring apologetically, 'I thought I was over the worst, but it springs up to hit me every now and then.'

'I know,' sympathised Fred, 'I feel the same

18

way about Tilly, my spaniel bitch. She got herself gored by the bull and Papa had to shoot her last week. I keep blaming myself for not taking more care. The silly creature doted on me.'

To James there was nothing incongruous about a comparison between his mother and a spaniel bitch. He nodded understandingly, gave a final wipe to his eyes, and turned the conversation. 'Has his lordship planned a route for us?'

Fred's sharp-featured face lit up. Bouncing over to the piano he struck a series of ecstatic chords. 'He has ... with the aid of the redoubtable Mr. Arthur Brookes, my revered tutor. They have been poring over the map of Europe every night after supper for a month. Dover, Calais, Paris, Montpellier ... Geneva, over the Alps to Italy, Turin, Rome, Naples, back via Germany and the Low Countries to Brussels. What fun' ... thump ... 'What indescribable fun' ... thump ... 'we shall have, you and I, Jemmy, on our Grand' ... thump ... 'Grand Tour!'

James could not help grinning at Fred's enthusiasm, although, remembering the Earl's letter, he felt bound to add a cautionary word or two. 'We are not meant to have fun, Fred ... well, not all the time that is. The tour is designed to be educational, is it not? Mr. Brookes will expect us to visit all the places of interest mentioned in the guide-books. We must take notes and measurements of buildings, and we must give our fullest attention to the words of the antiquarians in the museums and art galleries. We shall never again meet any people so knowledgeable about paintings and statuary and ... things.'

Over the top of the piano Fred was pulling a monstrous comical face, while with one hand he tugged his red hair into little tufts until it stood up all over his head like a garden broom. 'Lord save us, Jemmy, preaching don't suit you one bit. You ain't going to be a bore are you, dear fellow?'

James tried hard to keep his countenance, but it was very difficult with Fred playing the fool like that. He essayed one final plea. 'Fred, his lordship is paying all my expenses, and has expressed the wish that I shall do everything in my power to curb your high spirits. I am to use my best endeavours to exert a sobering influence upon you. It would, under the circumstances, be dishonourable of me to encourage any excesses of vitality on your part.'

Fred widened his eyes in mock alarm and moving away from the piano stuck both thumbs into the armholes of his yellow silk waistcoat. With shoulders bent, thin neck thrust forwards, and hands linked behind his back he paced the room, scowling ferociously, an accurate, if slightly exaggerated, imitation of the much put-upon Mr. Brookes.

'The case is far more serious than I had at first imagined,' he began, apparently addressing an unseen audience. 'My friend, Mr. James Darker, the person you now see before you, has turned pompous during the night. No visible signs of this horrid disease have yet manifested themselves, because the incubation period of the malady has only just begun. Three weeks, however, will suffice to reveal a certain lengthening of the facial proportions and a look of glassy pedantry in the eye for which there is no known cure. If the poor wretch is not too far gone a pitcher of cold water poured over his head, or the removal of his breeches in a public place might effect a partial cure, otherwise the only course to be pursued is to put him out of his misery with a shot-gun.'

Some sheet-music, flung indiscriminately at his head, stopped Fred in mid-flow and broke him up into laughter. Explosions of mirth mocked the serene dignity of William Darker's Music Room until the sound of carriage wheels abruptly cut them off. The two young men raced to the window. 'Grandmama!' gasped James, 'with Aunt Georgiana. They are come to supervise the packing of my trunks. Oh, Lord!' His face bore a look of peculiar desperation. 'They will stay to tea and supper and I shall have to shout down Grandmama's ear-trumpet, and Aunt Georgiana will keep on about foreign food, and Papa will rant on about Mr. Pitt and Mr. Wilberforce...'

Fred had him firmly by the arm. 'Let us run for it, dear fellow,' he urged. 'We can be out through the back kitchen, round to the stables and into my gig before Lady Branson has alighted from her carriage. Come on!'

James needed no second bidding. 'Did you know,' Fred asked breathlessly as they pelted into the stable-court, 'that the Prince of Wales is commissioning Henry Holland to extend his Palladian villa at Brighthelmstone? It is to be transformed into a veritable palace!'

'They say he is so deep in debt ... that he may be forced to put aside Mrs. Fitzherbert ... and marry someone approved by Parliament,' puffed James. 'Papa says that Mr. Pitt is willing to recommend ... payment of the Prince's debts ... if he will agree to marry a princess of the blood.

'Oh, Lord, another boot-faced German I suppose,' grumbled Fred.

The stable-boys, catching sight of Lord Frederick's long, gangling figure bearing down upon them, were already in process of harnessing the mare to the gig, and by the time James and Fred had climbed up they were almost ready for the off.

'Brighthelmstone is lately become very fashionable,' observed Fred as he took up the reins, 'ever since the renowned Dr. Russell advocated sea-water as a cure for all ills. In the last seven years or so the *bon ton* of London have turned it into their own private health resort and pleasure ground. When we come back from the Tour we must have a good sniff round there, dear fellow.' He laid a finger to his nose. 'Contacts, you know. With royalty about one never knows whom one might meet.'

The stable-boys stepped back, saluting the young lord and the young master respectfully, and handing up the former's whip, in return for which two silver coins were flipped in the direction of their grinning faces. A touch of the whip sent the mare flying forward, and as they shot out of the stable-court Fred roared, 'How about coming over to Penworth for a few rounds of fan-tan tomorrow evening? We can round up the Briggs-Watson boys and my Ralston cousins over at Heatherton Manor.'

James shook his head regretfully. 'Papa has arranged a supper-party for Mr. and Mrs. Houghton and Mary. I am to take my leave of my future wife and obtain her promise to wait for me until I return.'

Fred shot his friend a sharp look. 'Don't look so down-in-the-mouth, Jemmy lad. Anything can happen on the Grand Tour y'know. We might even get eaten by crocodiles!'

APRIL, 1790

James Darker takes leave of Miss Houghton

The Eating Room was filled to capacity. Grandmama Branson, Aunt Georgiana, Aunt Sophie—the latter with her husband and two strapping sons having been invited by William 'to make up the company'—shouted across the table at each other in deference to Lady Liz's affliction, while Mr. and Mrs. Houghton and their daughter Mary, heavily out-numbered by Darkers, Briggs-Watsons and Bransons, graced the beautiful walnut table with their slightly offended presences and took silent vows not to be 'brought round.'

It had come as a distinctly disagreeable shock to Mrs. Houghton when James had informed her of his plans to make the Grand Tour, her pride at the prospect of her future son-in-law journeying through Europe in the company of a lord doing battle with her disappointment that her only daughter was to remain a virgin for at least another twelve months. During that time any catastrophe might occur to prevent Mary's union with the only gentleman whose father had ever offered for her. My handsome son in return for your plain daughter and one hundred and fifty thousand pounds to seal the bargain. It was not at all a bad bargain when one mulled over the dismal alternatives open to poor Mary. Comfortable spinsterhood, or at best, marriage to a man three times her age who would drink and gamble her fortune away. With young Mr. Darker she at least stood a chance of enjoying a lively social life and of bearing half a dozen children to fuss over and occupy her days.

Mrs. Houghton felt out-classed and out-manoeuvred. She had not been able to insist upon the marriage taking place before James left for the Continent because the family were still in mourning for Mrs. Darker—not even the betrothal had been announced—and when she had hinted, with the greatest possible delicacy to Mr. Darker that she expected James to wed Mary immediately upon his return to England, that gentleman had stared at her frostily out of those small, grey-blue, codfish eyes of his and had demanded to know—truculently—whether she thought his son was capable of dishonourably breaking his sworn word. At this Mrs. Houghton had lapsed into affronted silence and the matter had not been referred to again.

Mr. Houghton, who had made his money out of silk-throwing in Derbyshire, said very little, leaving his wife to play the diplomat and taking an inward vow that if young James dared to jilt his daughter he should hear from him, by God he should. As for Mary, her thoughts were her own, though they were not perhaps so placid as might have been judged from the submissive eyes and the blank expression which she presented to the world.

James, for his part, surveyed the company from his mother's place at the bottom of the table and prayed only that the day should end, and that he might take his leave of Mary with as little embarrassment and fuss as possible. After supper he would take her out into the garden and murmur a few conventional phrases, enough to lull any suspicions she might have about his lack of feeling for her, and then he would speed her to her carriage with a thankful heart.

Aunt Sophie, his father's only sister, seemed to James to be dominating the supper-table conversation with tales of last season's hunting triumphs, commanding attention with the shrillness of her tone and the way her pale blue eyes darted from face to face to make sure that each member of the company hung upon her every word. A formidable, domineering woman was Aunt Sophie, who put the fear of God into her children and treated her inebriate of a husband with bullying contempt. I should take a bottle a day myself if I were married to Aunt Sophie, thought James.

The gentleman in question, Mr. Felix Briggs-Watson, was sitting between Augusta and Sarah, leering drunkenly at each girl in turn. Determinedly ignoring their troublesome uncle the two conversed brightly with Edward and Henry Briggs-Watson, their cousins, who sat opposite. James's roving glance fell upon Aunt Georgiana. That lady was patiently cutting up her mother's meat for ease of mastication. She reminded James vividly of his mother whose sister she was, except that Georgiana's face lacked the animation which had so enhanced Clarissa's claims to beauty. There had been another, younger sister, Aunt Ann, who had eloped back in the seventies, and whose name was never mentioned unless it was to deplore her flightiness and 'ingratitude.' Ingratitude for what, James had often wondered. She had probably been very beautiful. The ones who did daring things generally were.

James's wandering attention was engaged by the voice of Mrs. Houghton who was demanding to know—archly—if he should like to bring home to England some *objets d'art* to adorn his 'marital establishment.' Her insistence upon keeping the subject of her daughter's marriage well to the fore annoyed James as much as it did his father. He replied shortly, 'Not being an authority on *objets d'art*, Ma'am, I should hesitate to purchase anything which might be offered for sale by rogues and tricksters abroad. I am told the Englishman falls easy prey to such persons.'

'Indeed, sir?' Mrs. Houghton coloured and stabbed at her roast lamb. A sharp note of reproach enlivened her characteristically flat tones as she went on, 'I trust that you will not return *entirely* empty-handed. Mary would be *so* disappointed were she not to receive some little token of your travels ... and of your *affection*.'

It was a situation ready-made for Aunt Sophie, who loved to stir the pot. Her eyes gleamed wickedly. Having well digested the shades and nuances of the exchange, she put in quickly, 'James is discerning enough when it comes to choosing a pretty face. He'll not accept the counterfeit for that ... not *willingly* that is.' The remark was accompanied by a telling look at Miss Mary Houghton, who stared back at Mrs. Briggs-Watson without the least indication that she had taken offence.

Mrs. Houghton meanwhile bridled indignantly, and with a look appealed to James to defend his lady. Cursing Aunt Sophie under his breath James struggled to produce soothing words. 'A pretty face does not always go with a kind heart,' he managed. Aunt Sophie giggled into her wine-glass until silenced by a frown from her brother. William had no intention of allowing his sister to bait Mrs. Houghton to the point where she would break off the proposed match between her daughter and his son. A conversational lull ensued, during which the mounds of carved Scotch beef, roast lamb, Aylesbury duckling, dressed with lemon and rosemary and besieged with buttered

28

carrots and parsnips were disposed of. The melons, dates, figs and apricots were attacked with equal relish, as were the five varieties of cheese. The whole was 'seen off' with red and white wines of varying degrees of excellence and a potent liqueur which made the ladies confused and the gentlemen daringly bawdy.

Replete and discreetly belching into their table napkins, the company then sat back in their chairs to await the next predictable development in the evening's entertainment, presaged by William's overt signals to his eldest daughter that it was time for the ladies to retire. Smiling shyly Amelia rose and led the procession of slightly tottering ladies out of the Eating Room.

With well-practised efficiency the servants removed the used dishes and the white damask cloth, replacing these articles with a scoop of apples, a plate of biscuits and butter, and two decanters of port. The walnut table gleamed with the brilliancy of glass, reflecting the centre-piece of spring flowers, the brightly polished silver candelabra and the earnest, flushed faces of the gentlemen who looked forward to some interesting conversation now that the more refined ears of the ladies had gone. It was time for the men of the county to expand, to speak freely of the government's shortcomings, with an oath or two thrown in for good measure, to condemn the radicals, to toast Mrs. Dolly Jordan and Maria

Fitzherbert, to prescribe what was good for Holy Hannah More, and to recount, with a nod and a wink, their own exploits outside the bonds of matrimony.

Ranged in the sideboard were four silver chamber-pots so that the gentlemen might not be put to the inconvenience of interrupting their discourses by leaving the Eating Room for necessary purposes. All was set for a pleasurable two hours of rattle.

The talk turned once more to James's forthcoming tour, and the young man was pestered with requests for souvenirs. He was likewise besieged with advice. Mr. Thomas Nugent's Guide-Book was preferred to that of Mr. George Goss, for the latter contained phrases and imaginary dialogues not considered suitable for young gentlemen. Felix Briggs-Watson, having himself made the tour in '65, was listened to the most attentively, and enjoying the absence of his wife, who either ignored his opinions or silenced them with a few blistering words, waxed quite eloquent. 'Never travel by night, Jemmy,' he advised. 'Always be in your room before dark, and if you stay in an hotel, never forget to lock the door and to look behind mirrors and pictures for *hidden* doors. Dishonest inn-keepers are in the habit of robbing travellers at night by entering their chambers through some secret means of access.'

James suppressed a yawn. 'I believe we are to

stay in lodgings while we are in Paris, Uncle, and in Rome we are to reside with the Marchese di Ludovici, who is an acquaintance of the Earl of Adur.'

Mr. Houghton made a mental note to save up this tit-bit of information to convey to his wife. It might improve her temper to know that her daughter's elusive suitor was to be the guest of a high-ranking Italian nobleman. Meanwhile, Mr. Briggs-Watson, not a whit put off by his nephew's lukewarm reception of good advice, went on to list the things which must be taken note of. 'Flora, fauna, laws, customs and particularly,'—here a wavering forefinger was aimed at James—'military fortifi ... if ... cations. It is not incon ... inconseevbull,' pontificated Mr. Briggs-Watson drunkenly, 'that England will declare war on France in the foreseebull future, and such informayshun as you may glean could be of ines ... inesti ... mable value to the Brish ... British government.'

The finger continued to make jerky, stabbing movements, causing James to weave from side to side like a boxer parrying blows. 'Kesstions, Jemmy, keep askin' kesstions, that is the thing. Ask about fire pre ... precawshuns, mili ... military training, corp ... corpull pun ... punshmen, pay of clergy, the care of p ... pawpers, anythin' and evythin' y'ca think of, and c'llect prints and drawin's of evy place y'go to. Visit evy em ... em ...

31

emnent pers'nage y'can, and while travellin' through It'ly and Germ'ny 'ware of bandits. They haunt the woods'n highways, lyin' in wait for...'

James drank deeply of his port and determinedly closed his ears. He waited for several minutes, thinking his own thoughts to the background accompaniment of his uncle's slurred drone, and then, on the pretext of relieving himself, took a chamber-pot from the sideboard, disappeared behind the screen provided for the purpose—situated conveniently near the door—and made his escape. He still had to face up to the interview with Mary before he could lay his burning face and aching head upon a cool pillow.

His first idea had been to take his betrothed to the summer-house in the park, the former an unnecessary folly built three years previously by his father, but the deepening twilight and the cool, darting breeze made this course seem imprudent and he led her instead to the Morning Room, with its comfortable, unpretentious furniture, handing her to the scroll-ended sofa and seating himself beside her so that their bodies were almost, but not quite, touching. After a moment or two of embarrassed silence he began awkwardly, 'I shall only be away for a year, perhaps not so long. It largely depends upon the quality of the roads which I am told are very poor in Germany.'

'Yes, I know.' The hard angularity of her jaw, softened a little by the flattering glow of the candles, seemed to advance and recede before him. His eyes appeared to be slightly out of focus and he realised that he had drunk too much port. His tipsy state enabled him to observe her with less restraint than he had hitherto shown, and he noticed first of all her eyes. They were round, light brown, almost yellow in colour, expressionless as those of a prowling tiger. It was not too much to say that her stare, fixed and unwavering, repelled him. Her nose was flat and uneven, reminding him of the coloured aquatints of Queen Charlotte he had seen in Mr. Thomas's circulating library at Brighthelmstone. It was as uncompromising as the thin line of her unpainted mouth. Dark brown, frizzlated hair was surmounted by an ugly concoction of green silk ribbon bows. To this he was pledged for life.

Desperately he searched for something further to say, something which would bring a smile, however strained, to those tight lips and a light to the stone-like blankness of the eyes. 'I have imbibed a little too much port.'

'Oh.' She drew back a little and a sudden tide of anger washed over him. Was there nothing at all behind that hideous facade, no single redeeming characteristic which would make his future with her bearable, which would turn her into a human being? He remembered how

33

she had sat like a statue, allowing Aunt Sophie to insult her and refusing to bite back. 'Devil take it, Miss Houghton,' he muttered, allowing his exasperation to show, 'where are your *feelings*? I do not expect you to bear any affection towards me, for we are both the playthings of fate. We have been chosen for each other and may not marry for love, but if we are to live together we must conduct ourselves in a civilised manner. Do you not agree?'

Her mouth pursed into a small round O of disapproval. 'You, sir, are conducting yourself in a very *un*civilised manner. I find your attitude disagreeable in the extreme. As to my own feelings, I have never been asked by you until now to give expression to them. Ever since it was decided that we should marry you have kept as far away from me as is consistent with the undesirability of making your disgust for me obvious to all and sundry.' Suddenly those strange eyes of hers moistened, and her small mouth drooped at the corners. In that instant she looked so hideously vulnerable that he felt ashamed.

'Miss Houghton ... Mary,' he began uncertainly and tried to take her limp hand in his.

'No!' She snatched it away. 'Do not give me your pity, James. Do not break my pride as well as my heart.'

'Perhaps you would prefer to remain in your

single state rather than to marry me?' he suggested bluntly—and hopefully. No sooner were the words out of his mouth than he realised his mistake. Her thin lips stretched into the painful semblance of a smile. 'You have made up your mind then, that spinsterhood would be the only course left open to me if you were to disappear for ever out of my life?'

'No, no, you misunderstand me.' Hastily he sought to repair his error. 'I meant only that you might find the unmarried state preferable to being bound fast in wedlock to a man who cares nothing for you.'

He was being deliberately cruel now, for he knew, without a shadow of doubt, that he would be less than a man if he allowed himself to be carried along by his father's enthusiasm for the huge dowry that this girl would bring him. Somehow he must make her reject him so that she could withdraw from the bargain with dignity. 'Ours will be a loveless marriage,' he insisted.

'Loveless on your part, if you say so,' she returned, and now he thought he detected a hint of mockery in her eyes. 'Not on mine, I assure you. *I* love *you*, James. Not being the arbiter of my own fate I thought perhaps my father would choose to bind me to an old man, a widower with a brood of children whom I should be commanded to love as my own. When I discovered that the choice had fallen upon you I was in a positive ferment of delight. Fortune had smiled upon me in a way that I had never believed possible.

'He is handsome, I thought, and gentlemanly in his deportment, and together we shall beget children, and I shall be like every other girl in the county who makes a tolerably good match. I shall have nothing of which to feel ashamed, and I shall not have to play the spinster aunt and help with disagreeable children who are not my own and who laugh at me because I am not handsome, and therefore not worthy to bed with a man.'

For the first time he noticed how beautiful her hands were, white, with tapering fingers and perfect, oval nails. He noticed her hands because they were busy pleating the skirt of her yellow silk gown into tiny folds. She had not the least idea what she was doing so intent was she on her own outpourings. She was like a river rushing through the broken walls of a dam. He wanted to intervene, to forcibly restrain this totally unexpected and totally embarrassing purging of her soul and bring her back to the safe world of polite conventional exchanges, but the alcohol in his blood sapped his strength of purpose and anyway he had to admit to a certain fascinated interest in her words.

As she went on her face was half averted, reminding him of Amelia who had long ago established the trick of presenting her best side to the world. Here the scars were internal, but the intent to conceal was the same. 'Strange, is it not, that I had not thought how *you* would feel, James? I love you, therefore it stood to reason that you must love me in return, and would be as happy as I that our parents had come to such a sensible arrangement. It was only when I saw how you looked at me that I realised the true nature of your feelings towards me. I should have become aware of it before, of course. God knows, I had but to consult my mirror. I knew that Papa was having a difficult time in disposing of me. He often debated my future with Mama, speaking of me while I sat in the same room with them, as though I were an infant who had not the power of understanding.

'Every time Papa made one of his little speeches about me, bemoaning the fact that I was so plain, Mama would throw a fit of hysterics and rush me off to the hairdressers' establishment in Brighthelmstone, pleading with that foppish creature who owns it to arrange my hair in a *becoming* style. The present one would not do. It did not bring out the brightness of my eyes. It made my face look too long, my nose too flat. While Mama argued with the hairdresser I would stand there, endeavouring to stare him out of countenance, daring him to voice his thoughts which were plainly written upon his face. She is beyond redemption, this daughter of yours, Ma'am.

Why do you not resign yourself to the fact and have done?

'Knowing all this, enduring every possible humiliation which Mama could heap upon me, why, James, do you suppose that I deluded myself into thinking that you would feel any different from the hairdresser, that *creature* with his curled wig and his rouged cheeks?'

She paused, presumably to draw breath, and the silence in the Morning Room was long and terrible. His tongue clove to the roof of his mouth and he could not have spoken had his life depended upon it. Suddenly she swung round to face him, bright spots of colour staining her cheeks, proclaiming her anger. She said clearly, 'I shall not let you go, James. You have made your promise to marry me and I shall hold you to it. If you find me so abhorrent you must make shift to die in France or Italy, and I shall make a pilgrimage to spit on your bones.'

In the next instant she was gone, biting on her clenched fist to hold back the tears. Later, when he handed her to her carriage she gave him a brief, almost friendly smile, and he thought he knew how a fly must feel, caught in the toils of a spider's web.

*　　　*　　　*

Before he left for the Continent James strolled down to the churchyard in the village and walked, almost by instinct, towards the huge elm tree which had been rooted on the boundary beside the crumbling stone wall. There, hard against the wall itself, was the last resting place of one Patience Westlake, whose life had been abruptly terminated by the hangman in the year 1770. As children all the young Darkers had been drawn to this spot, as though by the pull of an invisible magnet, and had stood to gaze down and ponder the mystery which surrounded this one lonely tombstone standing well apart from all the rest. Cousin Patience had been hanged for murder. Whom had she murdered and why? What dark secret lay beneath the earth at their feet? The Darker children would often stay awhile to speculate and to shiver pleasurably before, in the manner of children everywhere, turning their attention to other more joyous pursuits. There were many in Piddingfold village who could have told them Patience's story, but none who dared, lest the wrath of William Darker descend on their heads. James knew that one day the secret would be revealed to him, but in some strange way he felt it was better not to know, for in the mystery lay also the excitement.

'Good-bye, Patience,' he said. 'I shall come and see you when I get back.'

MAY, 1790

An Adventure in Paris

On the day that James Darker took leave of his father he felt unaccountably depressed, but his flagging spirits were quickly restored by Lord Frederick who made an exciting adventure out of every incident which occurred between the time the small party left Dover and their arrival in Paris a fortnight later. Even the week spent at Dover waiting for a fair wind was passed in comfortable quarters in the 'Ship' inn, where the chamber-maids were accommodating and the landlord's smuggled brandy was declared by Fred to be the finest he had ever tasted.

Mr. Arthur Brookes, busy with his itineraries and guide-books, seemed not to notice the extra-curricular activities of his two charges as he happily estimated travelling times and distances and made copious notes concerning ruins, galleries, museums and sundry places of interest which 'must not be missed.'

Thirty-five, married and with five little Brookes's to feed, the reverend gentleman was delighted to have the opportunity of earning three times his normal stipend for the term of approximately one year. Not only that, but he would acquire a knowledge of foreign parts which could be of inestimable value to him in the future. Mr. Brookes's dream, long-cherished, was to open a school for young gentlemen, enticing to his doors the sons of wealthy merchants and professional men, the last-named category having in recent years become aware that a good education had its advantages. Already the printed prospectus rose in imagination before Mr. Brookes's enchanted eyes, 'Principal: The Reverend Arthur St. John Brookes, M.A. French, German and Italian a speciality. The Grand Tour made in 1790.' Mr. Brookes was a very happy man.

Having disembarked at Calais, James and Fred were convulsed with mirth at being searched for contraband, and watched with wicked glee as Mr. Brookes, under violent protest, removed his breeches, and a portly female of indeterminate age submitted with scarlet cheeks to having her stays investigated. The commissaires carrying out this enviable task were rough and thorough and reduced the lady to tears in very short order.

Fred, primed by his lordship, offered a substantial bribe for the rapid procuring of passports—an English passport not being recognised on the Continent—and they were on their way to the *Hotel d'Angleterre* within an hour of setting foot on French soil. Here they partook of Monsieur Dessin's *specialité de la maison*, fresh sea crabs and green salad,

41

and sampled the sparkling *Blanc de Blancs* Champagne.

Not having the least desire to explore the town of Calais, whose eight streets all converged on the market-square, and most of whose four thousand inhabitants went to bed at eight o'clock, the three gentlemen took to their beds, first having arranged with the landlord to rouse them in time to catch the nine o'clock diligence in the morning. 'We have thirty-two pieces of luggage,' Fred informed their host affably. 'They are counted.' The landlord stared at him long and consideringly, bowed and murmured, *'Oui, milord,'* and privately resolved not to overcharge this particular Englishman who spoke French like a native and whose pistol cases he had discovered to be unlocked.

Boulogne, Montreuil, Abbeville, Amiens, Clermont, Chantilly, St. Denis ... Paris. They made only one stop before entering the capital. This was at the insistence of Mr. Brookes, who declared that the Benedictine Abbey of St. Denis was on his itinerary and 'must not be missed.' Fred was about to protest, but gave in at a nudge from James, who produced his notebook with a flourish and out-stared his friend until the other followed suit. A predictable collapse into laughter ensued.

They saw the white marble sepulchres of the French kings, the effigy of King Henri II, crowned and robed, his noble features quietly composed, while below his recumbent figure yet another effigy of the dead king lay, in startling contrast to the one above. Here he was represented as a man, naked to the waist, his face contorted in agony from the lance-thrust which had penetrated his left eye and caused his death. The whole set piece was an object lesson in the transitoriness of life and the vanity of outward pomp. Even kings were brought low in the end and died as fearfully, and as painfully, as other men. A similar treatment had been given to the effigy of Anne of Brittany, wife of both Charles VII and Louis XII. The figure above was crowned and mantled, that below showed her straining against the pain of an incurable disease, with her head thrown back and her lips stretched taut across her bared teeth. So had this queen died. So would many die who looked upon her.

Sobered by these moralisings in stone the young men moved on with thoughtful sighs to admire Paolo Poncio's bas-reliefs of the victories of King Louis XII, and on again to marvel at the crown of Charlemagne. The very ordinary-looking sword of the Maid of Orleans sent the ardent Mr. Brookes into raptures, and it seemed that he could not write fast enough as the antiquarian droned through his long-established rigmarole. The tutor's sparse brown hair stood on end and his brown eyes sparkled with fervour behind his spectacles as he scribbled away, his ear cocked attentively so that he might not miss a single word. James dutifully followed his example, though with less enthusiasm, while Fred, disgracefully empty-handed, trifled with the exhibits, much to the annoyance of the antiquarian who objected vociferously when he picked up Joan of Arc's sword and playfully brandished it at James.

'Monsieur,' protested the elderly monk, who was disconcerted at being interrupted in mid-flow. 'That is a holy relic you make sport with. You will please to put it down.'

Fred, who admitted later to James that the thought of actually holding the Maid's sword had 'quite carried him away,' looked suitably abashed and relinquished the weapon. He asked conversationally, 'Did she ever kill anyone with that sword?'

The antiquarian looked shocked. 'Monsieur, she is a saint!'

'Yes, but she wasn't a saint during her lifetime, she was just a woman,' Fred argued cheerfully and illogically, 'and she did lead soldiers into battle. She must have killed *someone.*'

'I think not, Monsieur,' responded the old man severely.

'But she *must* have,' Fred insisted. 'She was wounded, or so the history books tell us. If she was wounded she must have been fighting.'

'Lord Frederick, *please,*' begged Mr. Brookes helplessly.

Fred shrugged and fingered the crown of Charlemagne. 'Oh, well, if everyone is going to be so dashed *touchy*.' He looked very young and stubborn, still unwilling, in spite of his eighteen years, to conform to the conventions of the adult world.

There were more formalities before the party of three could enter Paris, again dealt with by Fred by means of judicious bribes. Young men clamoured to offer their services as valets for fifty sols a day, flapping references through the windows of the diligence before the travellers had time to alight. Mr. Brookes waved them away. Fortunately he did not see the gestures which followed his retreating back.

Furnished rooms were secured in the Faubourg St. Germain, outside the old city walls, a four-roomed apartment for which they were charged seven guineas a week. 'Exorbitant!' exclaimed Mr. Brookes, looking around him at the shabby furnishings. Thankfully he left the formalities to Fred.

There followed a hectic week of sight-seeing, at the end of which Fred roundly declared that he had had enough. Standing at the window of their *salon* and looking down at the strollers below he announced, in the presence of James, his intention to rebel.

'We have seen every dashed painting in the Louvre, we have visited the Sorbonne, Notre Dame, Les Invalides, the Seine, the Champs-Elyéees and a score of churches and palaces; we have trudged the heights of Montmartre until our feet are on fire; we have taken measurements, made notes and drawings and listened to a lot of boring people telling us a lot of boring details which I, for one, have already forgotten.'

He swung round to face James, who was reclining on a sofa reading the '*Paris Matin.*' 'Dear fellow, do you feel like a little feminine company, a little bawdy entertainment?'

'No chamber-maids here,' said James lethargically, and suppressed a yawn.

'I was not thinking of chamber-maids.'

'What then?' James looked up in surprise.

'Professional whores,' explained his friend. 'Wiggy Russell made the Tour two years ago and he says there is a house in the Rue Neuve, near that odd little Huguenot church we visited yesterday...'

'St. Sebastian the Martyr,' put in James, airing his knowledge.

'...where,' Fred went on, loftily ignoring the interruption, 'for a fee of one hundred sols one may take one's pick of some very beautiful, very accommodating young ladies who can teach a simple gentleman to do things he never thought possible.'

James put down his newspaper. 'I am always willing to learn, Fred, as you very well know, but not at the cost of a dose.'

Fred roared with laughter. 'You don't know Wiggy Russell, dear fellow, if you think he would risk taking a dose. No, you may trust me, James. I shall lead you into scented, silken boudoirs and bring you out pure as the driven snow.'

'It's a bit late for that,' returned his friend, swinging his legs off the sofa. 'It is several months now since my cloak of virginity became muddy round the edges.'

'I should hope so, dear fellow. I soiled my cloak when I was twelve.'

*   *   *

The young men were at some pains to make their escape from the Faubourg St. Germain and the all-seeing, all-condemning eye of Mr. Brookes, who, alas, was not in the habit of retiring for the night before eleven o'clock. By dint of plying the unsuspecting tutor with rather more than his accustomed quantity of port, however, it was at last managed, and after assisting the reverend gentleman to bed the two conspirators tip-toed away and took carriage to the Rue Neuve. En route they were passed by a magnificently appointed carriage emblazoned with the coat-of-arms of some nobleman. By the light of a street lantern they could just make out a boar's head surmounting a ducal coronet. The conveyance was racing along at break-neck speed, preceded by two snarling mastiffs, who effectively cleared the way by snapping at the heels of anyone who dared to get too near. James whistled admiringly, 'Where can he be going at such a rate?' Fred smiled gently at such innocence. 'He is undoubtedly on his way to an assignation with a lady, dear fellow. She must be very beautiful indeed to merit such ardour.'

The house in the Rue Neuve looked eminently respectable, a tall, three-storey building with 'wedding-cake' decorations on its façade and a flight of steps leading up to a covered porte-cochère. It was situated in a terrace of eight similar houses, all of which looked as if they might belong to comfortable city merchants. There was one dissimilarity to this particular establishment, however, which immediately struck the eye of the least observant passer-by. Every window was fitted with a blind of red silk, behind which the light of chandeliers glowed pinkly, adding a subtle air of mystery which did not belong to sober, middle-class affluence.

Having mounted the steps a little ahead of James, Fred gave the brass bell-handle three vigorous jerks and fumbled in his waistcoat pocket for a scrap of paper given to him by the ubiquitous Wiggy Russell, and bearing testimony to the honesty and sound financial standing of one Lord Frederick Oliver, English gentleman. This was a very high-class establishment, as Fred had been at some pains to explain to his doubting friend James, he who had propounded the shockingly erroneous

48

theory that 'one whore-house is very like another.'

The door was opened slowly, and with admirable discretion, to reveal the short, cap-and-aproned figure of a young female who smiled politely and asked the gentlemen to state their business. Fred addressed her in his excellent French and produced his 'character-reference,' whereupon the two were invited into the carpeted vestibule and requested to '*Suivezmoi, s'il vous plait, Messieurs.*'

Without having time to notice much more than the predominance of the colour red, reflected in curtains, wall fabric and chairs, the two were conducted to a sizeable room opening off the vestibule which was furnished with a quantity of chairs in gilded wood and red plush and very little else, the only other item of furniture being a long mahogany table, upon which were neatly arrayed a variety of newspapers and periodicals. Crystal chandeliers were duplicated in a series of gilt-framed mirrors ranged along the walls.

Fred surveyed his surroundings with an air of amused wonder before dissolving into chuckles. A portrait of Diane de Poitiers hanging over the fireplace drew his attention. He walked over to study it. Naked to the waist, her head adorned with a pearled coif, this famous courtesan stared out at the world with the sweet and candid innocence of a Raphael Virgin.

'Apart from that'—Fred gestured with his thumb at the portrait—'I might very well be in the waiting-room of Dr. Collins, Papa's London physician. Do you know, dear fellow, we troop up to London in a body at the beginning of March, a pride of Olivers all eager to begin the new season, and our first port of call is at the house of Dr. Collins, into whose patient ear we pour the details of all our winter ailments and all our present symptoms, and we come away with our pockets bulging with pills and boluses, enough to last until our next visit.'

James smiled. 'We content ourselves with Mr. Frost, the Piddingfold apothecary. We have not had a qualified physician for some years now. Dr. Anderson was the last I believe. I say!' The exclamation was drawn from James as he caught sight of one of the newspapers reposing on the table. '"The Times," no less!' He picked it up and read aloud, '"Mr. Thomas Paine is to publish a defence of the revolutionaries in France."'

Fred sniffed. 'Fellow's a radical, what d'ye expect?'

'Mmm,' agreed James, his eyes scanning the print for any interesting snippets of information from England. He soon found one. 'Mr. Wilberforce is in full cry again. D'ye know, Fred, the Abolitionists have been something of a joke to father for more than twenty years now. In my opinion it is time he began taking them seriously.'

Fred nodded. 'It is only a question of time before a Bill goes through Parliament making the buying and selling of slaves illegal. There is nothing more certain, dear fellow. Within the next ten years I'd say.'

James was thoughtful. 'For myself, I think I shall choose Parliament as a career, if I can get a seat that is.'

'Papa might be able to help you there. He's got half the voters of Brighthelmstone and Arundel firmly in his pocket.'

James was just about to seize upon this interesting offer and explore its possibilities further when the door opened again to admit a middle-aged female attired in grey silk and white lace, who glided forward and without hesitation offered her hand to Fred. James stared at her with frank amazement, observing the starched muslin cap which sat upon the glossy black hair like a giant butterfly. Her face was long and pale and at first sight utterly devoid of cosmetics. Only the experienced observer might have detected the discreetly applied lip-salve and the touch of kohl on the eyelids which enhanced the colour of her innocent-looking violet-blue eyes. Her sober neatness reminded James of his Aunt Georgiana, but it was Georgiana with a subtle difference. His aunt was less composed, less sure of herself than this woman.

Fred took the offered hand and bowed, his usual friendly grin modified to a polite smile as he waited for the woman to speak. He saw that she carried in her other hand the piece of paper which he had given to the maid-servant. 'Lord Frederick, welcome to my house.' She spoke in English, her small mouth stretching into a warm, gentle smile of greeting. 'There was no need for this.' She allowed the piece of paper to leave her hand and float to the floor in a manner frankly theatrical and went on, 'Your friend, Lord Russell, wrote to me from London two weeks ago telling me that you were to be in Paris for a month, and that he would be greatly obliged if I would extend to you the hospitality of my house.' Her arms were flung wide in an all-embracing gesture. 'It is yours, my lord!'

James had the greatest difficult in conquering an insane desire to giggle, but took the cue from his friend who was exuding all the charm and courtesy of the English aristocrat. *'Madame, vous êtes tres gentil.'*

She bowed, and with a slight lift of her eyebrows indicated that the formalities were over. Time was money, and speaking of money ... another lift of the black eyebrows and a delicate, winning smile. Matching the extravagant gestures of his hostess Fred produced his pocket-book with a flourish and three hundred sols changed hands. Judging by the smile on Madame's face it was clearly enough.

Fred thought it high time to introduce

James. 'Madame, allow me to present my companion, Mr. James Darker.'

The beautifully cold eyes made a rapid survey of the other gentleman and placed him with deadly accuracy into the rank of middling gentry. She inclined her head with a condescending air not lost upon Fred. 'Mr. Darker is my very *good* friend,' he remarked significantly. She took his meaning at once and melted sufficiently to accord James a brief and business-like smile. 'Gentlemen, permit me to show you to your rooms.' So saying, she turned towards the door. James and Fred exchanged slightly startled glances and like two boys in the wake of the school housekeeper, obediently followed her out into the vestibule, up the red-carpeted staircase and along a dimly lit wainscoted corridor.

The woman stopped before a door upon which the numeral five was painted in gold, and having opened it a fraction, without bothering to knock, took James by the arm and gently urged him through the narrow aperture. The young man gave a little jump as the door closed softly behind him and he was left standing with his back to it, feeling rather foolish. The silhouette of a female figure, outlined against the red window-blind, immediately engaged his attention. He had never before seen a naked woman. His furtive love-making with Susannah and assorted English chamber-maids had always taken

53

place in the dark, amidst a jumble of raised petticoats and hastily removed under-garments, and his youthful impetuosity had been such that copulation was scarcely more than an animal act performed in the shortest possible time.

She moved towards him, gliding over the floor, skirting the enormous satin-draped bed which dominated the room, and came to stand before him, so close that the tips of her rouged breasts brushed his frock-coat, and his trembling knees made contact with hers. She was smiling at him, her head tilted a little to one side as if she sought to read his approval, as though to be approved of was very necessary to her. She was extremely beautiful, her complexion smooth and creamy, reminding him unromantically of the texture of fine kid gloves, her eyes dark brown and inquiring above a small, perfectly proportioned nose and a warm, inviting mouth. She moved even closer to James, rubbing herself against him and then quickly withdrew, leaving him feeling a little dizzy. She went and lay down on the bed, supporting herself on one elbow as she turned to look at him and caressing her own body with the fingers of her other hand.

James never knew how he managed to remove his clothes, an operation made even more difficult by her cool, investigative regard, but at last he was on the bed beside her, his hands reaching out for the smooth roundness of her body. She slid from his grasp and manœuvred her body until she lay on top of him, whereupon she commenced a gentle up and down sliding movement, using her nipples like probes to invade the tenderest parts of his anatomy, teasing him with her silky hair. He made small animal sounds until his rising excitement became unendurable and he took her savagely, which was as it should be, for she had done her whore's work well. Searching and thrusting, proud of the strength that surged through him, telling himself that he was strong enough to devour her, that he was lion-like in his mastery of her, he reached heights of ecstasy he had never known before, and knew he never would again without paying for the privilege.

During the ensuing hour they were together she aroused him twice more with tricks and devices well beyond the range of his limited experience. He rose from the bed exhausted, drained of all feeling, and like an automaton began replacing his clothes. Never again would he look at a woman, respectable or otherwise, without wondering how she would be in bed.

James was in the process of buttoning his waistcoat when the sound of a disturbance, not too far away, captured his attention. A man's voice, raised in anger, was drowned by the high-pitched scream of a woman hurling abuse. The man's voice was undoubtedly Fred's. Snatching up his frock-coat, and without so much as a backward glance at the promoter of his recent delights, James made for the door. As he opened it a figure flew past him, hotly pursued by an enraged individual who, catching sight of James, shouted to him to 'Come *on*, Jemmy. We've been cheated!'

James did not feel in the least cheated. He nevertheless caught the exciting spirit of the chase and joined in the pursuit with zest. The quarry was secured about halfway down the main staircase and was sent catapulting to the bottom with a well-aimed kick in the small of the back delivered by Fred. The sound of opening doors and questioning voices could now plainly be heard.

'What the devil, Fred ...?' James clung to the other's arm as they descended the remaining stairs to the vestibule. Fred was almost speechless with fury. His red hair stood on end and his normally pale cheeks were suffused with colour. A small dribble of saliva ran from one corner of his wide, extravagant mouth. He pointed an indignant forefinger at the stirring figure sprawled at the stairs' foot. 'It's a man!' he spluttered. 'That false bitch of a Madam gave me a man to bed with!'

James could hardly believe his ears. Slowly he lowered his bottom on to the penultimate tread and with his hands covering his face gave way to silent, shaking laughter.

The lady in grey made her appearance in the vestibule, frowning with Gallic disapproval at this unseemly disturbance in her smoothly-run house. Fred pounced on her and hissed a stream of rapid French into her ear. Momentarily she recoiled from Anglo-Saxon earthiness before replying sharply and at some length to the client's unjust accusations. James, whose French was of the schoolroom, caught the words 'Russell' and 'pederast' and looked up to see Fred going hot and cold by turns and making violent gestures of denial. The word 'Russell' was repeated several times.

By this time the young person on the floor had struggled to his feet, straightening his blonde wig, and endeavouring to restore his dishevelled attire to a semblance of decency. He was swearing loudly and appealing to Madame to compensate his lost dignity by throwing the English milord out into the street. Meanwhile, the English milord was hotly demanding his money back, while at the same time explaining to James that that damned villain Wiggy Russell had written to Madame telling her that his very good friend, Lord Frederick Oliver, preferred the company of boys to that of young ladies.

James, struggling manfully to keep his countenance, was quite unable to reply. Madame Bellecœur, for such was her unlikely name, was trying to persuade Fred to start again, this time with a young lady whom he might personally select from among her 'staff.' Fred, thoroughly put out, declined the generous offer and again demanded the return of his money. Madame did not haggle. She inclined her head in graceful acceptance of the inevitable and requested that milord would accompany her to her office. James, too weak from love and laughter to do anything except sit down, waited in the vestibule while the house gradually settled down and the clients concentrated on getting their money's worth.

On the way back to the Faubourg St. Germain, a distance of about half a kilometre, which the young men decided to cover on foot, James could not resist recounting his own amazing adventure. Fred was generously pleased and shrugged aside his friend's doubts about the ethics of permitting Lord Adur to pay for his pleasure. 'Stick by me, dear fellow, and you'll always be served wi' the best,' he apostrophised grandly.

Once more James began to laugh. 'What did the young gentleman do to you?'

'Not a thing,' came the quick rejoinder, 'though I must admit it was a close shave. I thought it was a young lady, you see. Deuced fellow was stretched out on the bed, fully dressed, and ogling me fit to bust. He suggested we share a bottle before getting down to business and I agreed, though I was quite anxious to make a start.' He added with a grin, 'It was as well I did, because as soon as the drink loosened his tongue he revealed all as they say. Of course, he thought I knew, but he pretended to be a woman because he imagined it would please me ... make the whole thing more exciting I suppose.'

'You were offered a lady afterwards,' James pointed out.

'Couldn't work up the appetite after that terrifying experience, dear fellow. Tell you what though, when I get my hands on Wiggy Russell I'll break his ducal line for him!'

MAY, 1790

A Visit to Versailles

A visit to Versailles was another 'must' on the busy itinerary of the indefatigable Mr. Arthur Brookes, and neither James nor Fred were averse to seeing the French Royal Family in the flesh. Such an experience might provide a good deal of suppertable conversation in the eating rooms of Frinton Park and Penworth Hall.

Since the storming of the Bastille the previous year the luckless Louis XVI and his consort, Queen Marie Antoinette, had become, so to speak, the property of their unloving subjects, and the halls and corridors of all the royal palaces echoed and re-echoed to the determined thumpings of hundreds of peasant feet. Red-bonneted, loud-voiced and

59

menacingly belligerent, the people of France invaded the royal apartments and addressing their monarch as 'Citizen Capet' probed inquisitively into his day-to-day routine, while offering advice as to the manner in which he should conduct his life. It was a sight not to be missed.

Strolling through the *Cour de Marbre*, our party of three gentlemen emerged on to the terrace and obtained an awe-inspiring view of the 1,800-feet long western façade of the palace with its 375 windows, all capturing the morning sunlight and winking back at them. 'Odd's fish,' exclaimed Fred, deeply impressed, 'our Farmer George has nothing to compare with this.'

'Indeed, no.' Mr. Brookes was full of enthusiasm. 'This palace was built by King Louis XIV, the great Sun King himself.' Eagerly he consulted his guide-book and read aloud: 'The palace was erected with the inspired help of architects such as Louis Levau, J. H. Mansart, Le Nôtre, Le Brun and many others and became the seat of French government, housing as many as 10,000 of the nobility—and the gardens are among the world's most splendid showpieces. Gentlemen,' said Mr. Brookes, settling his spectacles more firmly on his nose, 'we must not depart without seeing the fountains. I have made an itinerary, *un petit tour*.' He giggled self-consciously. 'We shall commence with the

Parterres d'Eau and go on from there to the *Fontaines de Diane* and *du Point-du-Jour, Bassin de Latone* and the *Salle de Bal...*'

By this time Fred was already raising his eyes to heaven in despair and making frantic signals to James to put as much distance as possible between himself and the garrulous tutor. Observing his charges sidling away Mr. Brookes called after them, 'The palace first, gentlemen. The gardens and fountains may be visited later, after we have partaken of our noon meal.'

The chapel—'full of Roman ornamentation'—as Mr. Brookes described it, was visited first, after which the party ascended to the royal apartments on the first floor, trailing behind a noisy procession of people, who were conducting themselves in such a disorderly manner that Mr. Brookes quickly became alarmed. James and Fred, forestalling a possible retreat on the part of the tutor, took an arm each and briskly marched him up the wide marble staircase in the wake of a stout, heavily-built man waving a butcher's cleaver. Mr. Brookes, paling visibly, allowed himself to be propelled forward and lapsed into unhappy silence. The sight of Louis XIV's magnificent bedroom, situated in the exact centre of the palace, and overlooking the Cour Royale, and the adjoining *Galerie des Glaces*, restored his powers of speech, and he scarcely noticed the jostling crowds about him as he stared at the fantasies of an extravagant king, a little shop-soiled now by the many commoners who had passed through the palace. 'Stupendous,' he murmured, 'truly stupendous!'

'I had not bargained upon its being so dirty,' Fred remarked to James. 'Have they no servants to set things to rights? I declare, I am quite disappointed. Shabby splendour is the most depressing thing in the whole world.'

As they proceeded from room to room, the crowd seemed to grow quieter, as if anticipating some fascinating spectacle, until in the end only the sound of pattering feet could be heard, interspersed with the occasional cough. It was an eerie kind of non-silence which caused James and Fred to exchange puzzled glances. 'Something is up, you may be sure!' whispered Fred. What that something was soon became apparent, for as they passed through yet another elaborately ornamented door a scene confronted them which none would have given credence to had they not witnessed it with their own eyes.

They were now in the Queen's salon, a richly-appointed apartment containing elegant furniture of the finest sort. Chairs and sofas upholstered in blue satin brocade, fringed with gold, stood upon a blue hand-woven Chinese carpet which covered almost the entire expanse of floor. A pair of satinwood secretaires, crossbanded with rosewood and ebony inlay, stood against one wall and a huge circular walnut table, inset with porcelain medallions depicting the heads of the kings of France since Charlemagne, dominated the centre of the room. Upon the walls hung priceless paintings by some of the great sixteenth-century masters, among them Veronese's 'The Marriage of St. Catherine,' which hung over the white marble fireplace flanked by two ormolu candelabra. Pieces of silver and porcelain abounded, and a large mantel clock in ormolu, in the form of Cupid driving a chariot through the clouds, with butterflies as steeds, chimed the quarters and the half hours, sending forth silvery vibrations of sound very much in keeping with the sumptuousness of its surroundings.

All this was assimilated by the eyes of the visitors within a moment or two before they became aware of the small *tableau vivant* posed in the farthest corner of the *salon*. Wedged across the corner was what appeared to be a large mahogany desk or table, a vulgar, plebeian piece, totally incongruous among the other more delicate furniture, and behind this monstrosity stood the King and Queen of France, each holding a child by the hand. The children, a boy of five and a girl of twelve, looked up into the faces of their parents now and again, silently inquiring into the nature of this absurd ritual they were being forced to endure.

'God save us, they are *embattled* behind that table!'

Fred's low-voiced observation nudged Mr. Brookes into nervous expostulation. 'Hardly, my dear Frederick, hardly. It is a necessary precaution, I would judge, to prevent their coming into contact with the common herd.'

Fred shot him a look of indulgent cynicism. 'The Queen is *terrified*, that is quite plain to see. You have only to look at her eyes.'

James murmured agreement as they edged nearer to the Royal Family. The King and Queen were exchanging greetings with their passing subjects, replying to an assortment of remarks. 'Good-day to you, Citizen Capet, and to you, Citizeness.' 'You are looking well, Citizen, perhaps a little too fat, but that is because you eat too much.' 'Good-day, Citizeness, that is a very fine dress you are wearing. The cost of it would keep my family in food for a year. Never mind, soon we shall all be equal in the sight of God.'

Louis, heroically smiling, responded to this insulting barrage with apparent good humour. The Queen endured it with apparent calm and stoicism, although mixed with the terror in her eyes was another, quite violent emotion which James was quick to detect. He said, 'She is full of rage. She would like to spit upon those who taunt her.'

'How very ordinary-looking *he* is,' said Fred. 'He reminds me of Mr. Lovegrove, Papa's banker in Lewes. There is nothing in any way distinguished about his lineaments.'

They were speaking in English, their voices prudently lowered, but even so James glanced nervously about him, cowed by the threatening atmosphere, and anxious that none should understand their discourse. Suddenly, the man with the cleaver leaped out from the ragged line of his fellows and moved towards the frail bastion of the table. He was followed instantly by a score of others, who clustered about the table, eager to take part in whatever it was that their friend Pierre, the butcher, had in mind.

Fred and James, irresistibly attracted by the prospect of a dialogue between the sovereigns of France and their subjects, joined the small gathering, ignoring Mr. Brookes' agitated suggestion that they should move on. Outnumbered, two to one, the tutor made his way with cowardly speed to the ground floor, and from thence out into the gardens, where he drew in gulps of good, clean air and offered up a prayer that his young gentlemen would come to no harm.

Meanwhile, the butcher, addressing the Queen, requested that she would be so good as to lift up young Louis Capet so that the people might take a look at the heir to the throne. The Queen directed a look of horror at her husband. He smiled down at her reassuringly and leaning over picked up the Dauphin, holding the child before him for the crowd to see. Before the King could make a move to prevent it his son had been snatched from his arms and was being hoisted on to the broad shoulders of the butcher who then produced from the bosom of his blood-stained blouse a red woollen cap. Eager hands took it from him and the man lowered his immense bulk so that the cap might be placed on the child's head. This done, not without some difficulty since the child, plainly terrified, wriggled in all directions in order to avoid being touched by dirty peasant hands, the butcher straightened up and harangued the people.

'Citizens! Hear me! I bear upon my shoulders the future King of France. Shall he reign in the despotic manner of the old Valois and Capets?'

'No!' the crowd roared back predictably. The brawny arms of the butcher waved them to silence. 'No, he shall not, my friends. He shall be educated as a child of the people. He shall be taught how to hew wood and to mend his own shoes, and to butcher his own meat. *I* shall teach him that!' The cleaver, now stuck in his belt, was removed and flourished. It sliced through the air dangerously near the Dauphin's head and the Queen gave a little scream. Louis stifled it with a hand clamped firmly over her mouth. The mob enjoyed the spectacle of their King disciplining the German woman and voiced their approval. 'That is the way, Citizen. Clap on the bridle!'

The butcher's voice rose above the laughs and jeers, clamouring for their attention.

66

'Louis Capet shall be put among the peasants in the fields and made to till the soil until his back is breaking, and then, if he has done his share he shall be given black bread to eat and thin red wine to drink, but only if he has done his share, otherwise he shall be sent to bed without his supper, so that he may learn that a man may not eat if he cannot work, so that he may be like us, citizens, and know the aching pain of a starving belly!'

The butcher was warming to his theme. With a fine sense of the dramatic he arched his back and thrust forward his hands, like a wrestler waiting to get a hold on his opponent. Though the hair on his head was brown his body hair was reddish in colour; it grew thickly on his chest, on his back, on his arms and legs and on his large red face which had not seen a razor for three days. As he moved, the sun, slanting through the tall, round-headed mullioned windows, played upon those hairs, turning them to gold, transforming an ordinary butcher into a satyr, half-man, half-beast. His hearers fell silent, hanging upon his next words, willing slaves to the spell of one who had set himself, by the sheer power of his personality, above them. Few of them realised that this was the way the system they so hated had originated in the first place. So had the first King of France swayed the multitude—with words—and with the strength of his sword-arm. So had he been invested with the mysterious symbols of kingship.

The butcher's voice was now well modulated, for he sensed that he had them in the palm of his hand. 'His feet shall be left unshod, so that he may feel the soil and the stones of France torturing his flesh, and his heart will be moved to pity for all those who have not enough money to spare to buy themselves a pair of sabots. He shall be taught to read, but only those things which it is good for him to know shall he be allowed to learn from his books. He shall be brought to the States-General to hear the words of our leaders, Citizens Necker and Lafayette, and none shall bow the knee to him, for he will be one of us, citizens, one of us!'

The roar that succeeded these words could be heard from one end of the palace to the other. Arthur Brookes heard it as he wandered miserably towards the fountains, and shivered with apprehension. Fred and James, now firmly entrenched among the mob, clung tightly to each other, the former markedly devoid of his normal gay, insouciant air. Wisely, they refrained from speaking. The Dauphin, weeping for his mother, was handed back to her, along with yet another red cap which Citizeness Capet was loudly commanded to place on her head. She did so, her hands trembling visibly, and the people voiced their approval yet again. 'It suits you, Citizeness. It makes you look more like one of us.'

'Where is Madame Elizabeth?' a shrill female voice demanded suddenly. 'Does she think herself too good to meet the people of France?' Madame Elizabeth was King Louis's sister.

The cry was taken up, while Louis, endeavouring to make himself heard above the rising tumult, excused his sister on the grounds that she was suffering from a severe chill.

'Fetch her!' screamed the woman. 'Let us see for ourselves that you do not lie, Capet.'

The King, after a hurried word of reassurance to his wife, emerged from behind the table. A pathway was grudgingly cleared for him and he strode with calm, measured steps out of the *salon*. 'Five minutes, Capet!' another female voice yelled after him. 'If you are not back within five minutes we shall come and get you.'

The attention of the mob, ominously increasing in size with the passing of each moment, was now focused entirely upon the unfortunate Queen. With her children clinging to her skirts she stood as if turned to stone, looking straight in front of her. One or two women edged their way forward and reaching out, touched her dress, pulling at the blue satin bows which decorated the front of her bodice. One began tugging at the lace on her sleeve until the delicate fabric parted company from the cream satin to which it was attached. Yet another grinning harridan leaned over the table and with lighting swiftness produced from the pocket of her apron a pair of scissors. With these she snipped off a lock of hair from the head of the little princess. The child shrieked and hid her face in her mother's skirts. The crowd murmured, beginning to smell blood.

Marie Antoinette turned her head in quiet desperation towards the direction from which her husband must come with Madame Elizabeth. A slow tear trickled down her cheek. Fred, who was standing directly in front of her now, inched forward a little, with James still clinging firmly to his arm, and with piercing clarity yelled, 'Citizens! There is no sport here among this clutch of Capets. Who is for a look at the fine horseflesh in the stables and a long piss in the fountains?' With his usual incredible penetration he had sounded exactly the right note. There was a brief moment of silence followed by a yell of surprised laughter and a general stamping exodus through the door leading to the corridor and staircase. The Queen was staring at Fred with eyes opening wider every second. Swiftly she leant towards him and whispered, 'You are English, Monsieur?'

Fred mouthed the words *'Oui, Majestie,'* and with a gesture so rapid that James was not quite certain whether he had seen it or not, she transferred something from her own hand to

70

Fred's. At the same time she spoke a couple of sentences and then drew back. The whole exchange had taken but a moment and then the two young men were on their way out of the *salon*. As they left they passed the returning King, who was accompanied by a small, fair young woman. Madame Elizabeth, pale as death, clung to her brother's arm as if her life depended upon it. Louis was looking about him with an air of surprise and, thought James, of enormous, heartfelt relief.

*   *   *

They came upon Mr. Brookes sitting beside the *Bassin d'Appollon*, his thin face set into lines of melancholy resignation. He greeted his charges with undisguised warmth. 'My dear young sirs, how very happy I am to see you.'

Fred laughed. 'Did you think that big fellow with the cleaver had got us, Brookes?'

Mr. Brookes did not appreciate the jest. 'I feared, yes, I greatly feared that something untoward might have befallen you, Lord Frederick,' he said severely, 'and you will please to remember in future that I am responsible for your continued good health. If anything should happen to you I should be required to answer for it to his lordship. I am also responsible for Mr. Darker,' he added rather belatedly, an afterthought which made James chuckle.

When informed that Fred had a private audience with Their Majesties later on that same evening, Mr. Brookes was suitably impressed, not to say astounded. 'So that is what it was all about,' James murmured.

Fred felt in his waistcoat pocket and produced a ruby ring shaped like a star. 'I am to give this token to a lady who will come down to the small courtyard in front of the *Hotel des Pages* on the north side of the palace,' he said. 'We had better go and locate it now, in order to avoid wasting time later on. You, Jemmy, are to come with me. Her Majesty specifically said "and your friend".'

James was flattered. 'I have never been introduced to royalty before.'

'You will find it a sobering experience, dear fellow,' replied Fred. 'You may take my word for it that they are very much as other people, except that they are apt to speak a little more loudly. That is to make sure that their every word is taken down by someone for the benefit of posterity.'

They spent the rest of that day touring St. Germain in a *coche*, an uncomfortable public conveyance which rattled their bones and raised red welts on the skin of their posteriors.

Mr. Brookes declared his intention of going once more to the Saint-Chapelle. 'A Gothic jewel!' he enthused. 'Did you know, gentlemen, that it contains the most ancient stained glass windows in Paris? Eleven hundred and thirty scenes from the Bible are depicted in colour. It was built specially by St. Louis to house the True Crown of Thorns which he purchased from the Venetians.'

Thankfully, James and Fred despatched Mr. Brookes back to the centre of Paris and after having refreshed themselves with bread, cheese and red wine purchased from a wayside vendor, made their way back to Versailles.

Their escort, a petite, extremely pretty young woman, bade them welcome and conducted them back to the main building and to a little door in the corner of the *Oeuil de Boeuf* which opened upon the service room for footmen and other liveried servants. Here cupboards and padded benches lined the walls; stretched out upon the latter were one or two servants, sound asleep and snoring loudly. A maze of small uncarpeted passages led eventually to the wide, carpeted corridors of the King's apartments which lay on the opposite side of the palace to those visited by the young men in the morning.

The first thing that struck James and Fred was the total difference in the atmosphere to that previous nightmare visit. Gone were the commoners, who still permitted themselves to be excluded after the hour of five o'clock, and in their place were a series of soft-footed servants, bearing candelabra from room to room, or gliding along armed with long poles which they used to close out-of-reach windows. There was an air of calm gentility about these comings and goings which formed so strange a contrast to that other mad stampede of the morning that the two could hardly believe they had actually witnessed such terrible scenes.

The King and Queen were waiting in the former's *salon*, Louis playing upon the harpsichord, Marie Antoinette busy with a large piece of tapestry which she had draped over her lap. In the moment before she looked up, having heard the *Marechale de Chambre* announce the visitors, James surprised an expression of insufferable weariness upon her small, neat features. Her large, intensely blue eyes lit up at the sight of the two young men and her face assumed an expression of such bright cordiality that James surmised it to be some months since anyone 'friendly' had visited Versailles. The mutilated gown of the morning was gone. She was now wearing a creation of blue velvet trimmed with sable, the bodice banded with a dozen or more rows of pearls, the sleeves bordered with lace. More pearls were entwined in her hair, and hanging from her ears were large pearl drops. She looked like a china figurine.

The King stopped playing and stepped forward with alacrity to greet them. He was obviously deeply touched when Fred knelt on one knee before him, kissed his hand and announced his own name and title. James

74

followed suit, feeling distinctly awkward, and then the process was repeated before the Queen, whose eyes looked suspiciously bright. So reduced in state were the King and Queen of France that they now permitted commoners to sit in their presence, and chairs being sent for and brought forward by liveried flunkeys, the two were soon comfortably ensconced and waiting for royalty to open the conversation.

With a graceful gesture of her hand the Queen indicated Fred and informed her husband that this was the young gentleman who had rescued her from the unwelcome attentions of the mob. She spoke in English, a concession to their nationality which would have been unthinkable a year ago. Fred blushed fiercely and apologised for the necessity of using language which would, in normal circumstances, have been unforgivable in the presence of Her Majesty.

Louis waved this aside as unimportant— Her Majesty had heard worse in the last twelve months—and leaning forward, with his hands clasping his knees, inquired eagerly if His Majesty King George had been informed of the terrible state of affairs now existing in France.

Fred was at some pains to conceal his astonishment. 'Your Majesty, surely our ambassador has kept you *au fait* with the thoughts of our people in London?'

Sadly, Louis shook his head. 'I have not seen

the English ambassador for at least six months, Lord Frederick. He is not permitted by the revolutionaries to come into my presence. All his dealings are with the States-General. You would greatly oblige me by answering my question.' A touch of regal impatience in this last. Old habits die hard.

'Sire,' Fred said earnestly, 'my father was at the English court three months ago and found His Majesty greatly distressed by the storming of the Bastille and the subsequent terrible events. I do not believe, however, that His Majesty has any idea of the indignities to which Your Majesties are subjected within your own palace.'

'Ah,' sighed the King, 'it is a sad spectacle, is it not, Lord Frederick, to see a King at the mercy of his subjects?'

'Indeed it is, Sire.' Fred looked down at his feet. It was not only a sad spectacle, it was a horribly frightening one. The Queen startled him by asking, 'Is there any talk of England declaring war against France?'

Fred hesitated. This was dangerous ground. James, watching his friend, marvelled at his cheerful aplomb. This was a different person altogether from the lively young man who was always ready for a new escapade. 'I think, Madame,' Fred began carefully, 'that there is no possibility of that at the present time. It is fervently hoped in Great Britain that the troubled times in France will pass, and that

76

Your Majesties may be able to work out some form of government acceptable to the more radical elements in your kingdom.'

It wasn't bad for a lad of eighteen. Louis must have thought so too, for he looked at Fred with a new intentness of regard which the other found slightly disconcerting. 'Will you be willing, Lord Frederick, to take a message to King George for me? When do you return to England?'

Fred was so flustered by the first question that he plunged confusedly into answering the second. 'I . . . not for at least . . . Your Majesty, we are to go on to Switzerland, Italy and Germany . . .'

'About a year?' Louis suggested helpfully.

Fred nodded wordlessly. 'Then perhaps if I dictate a letter to my secretary, you will carry it about your person until you can avail yourself of an opportunity to send it on to London?'

'I shall be honoured, Sir.'

Louis rose and departed without another word. For the first time James noticed that there were no ladies or gentlemen in attendance. Pondering this phenomenon he came to the conclusion that discretion on the part of Their Majesties had occasioned this peculiar omission.

The Queen cut across his thoughts with, 'And what is your profession to be, sir, after you have completed your travels?'

'I hope to go into Parliament, Your

Majesty,' James answered nervously.

Her smile was ever so slightly mocking. 'Ah, yes, that is the place where the King of England is instructed by his people as to what he must do in order that they shall lend him money.'

'The King is *advised* by his Parliament, Madame,' replied James before he could stop himself.

Her well-marked brows rose a fraction. 'And does His Majesty always take the advice of his Parliament?'

'I believe so, Madame. In most cases anyway.'

'Would they take away his liberty if he did not?'

Fred intervened with a light laugh. 'That would be a somewhat drastic measure, Madame.'

'But it has been done before in England, has it not?'

A long silence ensued, during which the Queen placidly plied her needle and James and Fred studied their hands. Nothing more was said until the King returned bearing a sealed letter which he handed to Fred. After kind expressions and good wishes for the rest of their tour the two young men were shown out.

Back at the Fauborg St. Germain Fred extracted the letter from his pocket and placed it carefully upon the table, eyeing it much as he would have done a squib which was liable to go off at any minute. Then he went to fetch his tinder-box, and before the startled eyes of his friend produced a spark with which to ignite the letter. 'Do not look so shocked, dear fellow,' he admonished James. 'This is not the first time that inflammatory correspondence has lived up to its name.' He wagged a finger at James. 'Lesson Number One, never get embroiled in the politics of a foreign power. It is far too dangerous. You and I must forget all that has passed this evening and Mr. Brookes need not know that our audience with the King and Queen was anything more than a pleasant exchange of conversation.' He smiled gently. 'Dear fellow, what I like about you most is your charming innocence.'

'I felt sorry for them,' mumbled James.

'And I,' returned Fred quickly, 'but how is one to help a woman who, despite all her present misfortunes, still sneers at the idea of constitutional government?'

JUNE, 1790

Amelia Darker is spoken for

On a bright morning in early June the Darker family sat at breakfast, enjoying the feeling that summer had come at last. According to the custom of the last few weeks the girls began to wonder aloud as to 'dear James's whereabouts' and to bemoan the fact that he was such an infrequent letter-writer.

'Letter-writing is for females,' William declared, spreading his toast lavishly with butter. 'It is no wonder to me that most of the novels you girls read are written by females. The fair sex are well practised in the art of putting pen to paper and churning out sentimental rubbish.'

'Oh, Papa,' protested Amelia, always the one who was willing to do battle with William's stubborn opinions, 'Miss Fanny Burney is considered to be a very fine novelist. Dr. Johnson is said to have praised her work very highly.'

'Indeed,' replied her father sourly, punctuating his speech with brisk flourishes of the butter-knife. 'I consider that to be no recommendation at all, miss. I met the fellow once at Brooks's Club, about fifteen years ago it was. A more arrogant, self-opinionated bladder of lard it has never been my misfortune to bandy words with. Thought a lot of himself because he was touched for the evil by Queen Anne when he was a child. Says he can remember a tall woman with something black on her head, and the sound of a child crying somewhere. Not the Queen's child, of course. She was long past child-bearing by then, and anyway, George of Denmark had been dead for years.'

Amelia fell silent. It really was no use

80

arguing with Papa. He always had the last word upon any subject and a maddening habit of turning the conversation right away from the matter under discussion.

Caroline and Elizabeth, the two youngest Darker girls, were exchanging views on the shortcomings of Miss Parrish, their long-suffering governess. 'She is *mean*,' declared ten-year-old Caroline, spooning marmalade on to her side plate. 'She says I am to copy out my essay on the trades of London again because my writing looks as though a spider has crawled across the page.' A large bite of toast muffled her next words. 'I shall *not* do it and she will burst into tears and declare that I have given her the megrims.'

'You *shall* do it again,' Amelia told her severely. 'If you do not there will be no outing to Brighthelmstone on Thursday to see the foot-races on the Steine.'

Caroline pouted. 'You are mean too, Milly.'

'That is quite enough from you, miss,' William intervened, 'and you will show the essay to *me* when you have finished. If I do not consider it well enough it shall be done yet again.' His gaze abruptly transferred itself to Amelia. 'I have had an offer for you, my dear.'

Augusta and Sarah stared at their father as if he had suddenly announced his intention of flying to the moon. Amelia sat very still, an icy trickle of fear crawling round her stomach. 'An offer, Papa?' she repeated quietly.

'From Sir Edward Mulliner,' replied her father.

Augusta made an involuntary exclamation of protest. 'Oh, but Papa, Amelia could not ...' She went bright red, lowered her head and sneaked a miserable glance at her sister. Under the table Sarah reached for Amelia's hand. William went on as though nothing had happened. 'Sir Edward, as you know, is a very good friend of mine. He has been a widower now for ten years and his children are all flown from the nest.'

'He is a *grandfather*, Papa,' Amelia said. 'His eldest grandchild is the same age as Elizabeth.'

Eight-year-old Elizabeth giggled. Sarah shushed her with a look.

'It is true,' William continued imperturbably, 'that Sir Edward is of mature years, but he is a very wealthy man, and you can scarcely look to do better, Amelia.'

Amelia's hand flew to her face, and as if in response a shaft of pain sliced through her unequal leg. 'I think I should rather remain unmarried, Papa,' she said carefully.

'And *I* should rather you married,' returned her father, wiping his mouth with his napkin. He laid aside the snowy square of damask and picked up a small hand-bell which he rang with unnecessary vigour. Elise, the coloured parlour-maid, answered the summons and going to the sideboard began to pour the hot chocolate. William leaned back in his chair and examined his daughter's face for signs of outright rebellion. One could never be sure with Amelia. She'd be meek as a kitten one moment and spit like a jackal the next. If only the girl could be brought to realise what a miserable future lay in store for her if she rejected the one offer she was ever likely to get and opted for spinsterhood instead. He said with forced cheerfulness, 'I have asked Sir Edward to be good enough to drive over for tea this afternoon. The sooner you get to know each other the better. Now do not look at me as though I have given orders for your execution, Amelia. It is not as if I am rushing you into anything. You may not marry for at least six months yet, because of your poor dear Mama, so you will have plenty of time to grow comfortable with Sir Edward.'

William's sharp tone indicated that his final word upon the subject had been said, and the meal was completed in unhappy silence. Even Caroline and Elizabeth looked subdued, and kept darting curious glances at Amelia. Their eldest sister had all at once become an object of peculiar interest to them.

Up in the bedroom which she shared with Sarah Amelia at on the edge of the bed and stared unseeingly at the exotic birds decorating the pale green wall fabric. The room had once belonged to Aunt Sophie, who had early developed a taste for *Chinoiserie*. It was more the rage now than it had been twenty years ago.

Aunt Sophie had always been well in advance of her times. Amelia was not often given to weeping, for she had learned very early in life that it solved nothing. Its therapeutic use for easing the tension produced by wretchedness she would have considered an indulgence.

'What in heaven's name shall I *do*?' she asked herself now. 'If Papa is determined upon this match I can see no means of escaping from it.'

After sitting thus for twenty minutes or so, fruitlessly brooding, Amelia came to the conclusion that the only cure for wretchedness was action. She therefore got up, and taking her bonnet and pelisse from the wardrobe, donned these articles with her usual economy of movement. A pair of gloves, a reticule and a parasol completed her ensemble, and with these articles all firmly in place she descended to the ground floor and repaired to the Morning Room, where she informed her father that she intended to walk down to the village to purchase some orange-flower water from the apothecary's shop in the High Street.

William, who was pretty open-minded about his daughters' comings and goings, nodded assent and disappeared behind his copy of 'The Times,' on the back page of which Amelia caught a glimpse of an advertisement for 'Mr. John Bennett's gold watches in return for one guinea.'

Various ear-splitting and discordant sounds

coming from the direction of the Music Room indicated that Sarah and Augusta were preparing themselves for their weekly music-lesson, given by Mr. Tidy from Newporth, who would arrive punctually upon the stroke of nine and depart as promptly—and without a doubt gratefully—upon the stroke of ten, for Mr. Henry Lambton's house half a mile away. There, two more young and aspiring female musicians awaited him in the shape of Mr. Lambton's daughters Charlotte and Mary.

Thankfully Amelia left her sisters to it. Not being possessed of a musical ear herself she had managed to persuade William that she would be wasting a great deal of his money were Mr. Tidy to devote his time and services to her.

Half an hour after leaving Frinton Park Amelia entered the shop of Mr. Robert Frost, the Piddingfold apothecary. The gentleman in question had come to the village three years ago, after the sudden demise of Dr. Anderson, and had physicked the inhabitants of that part of the county with such skill and success that people wondered why they had ever bothered to pay high fees just for the privilege of being looked at by a member of the Royal College of Physicians. An added bonus was the fact that Mr. Frost diagnosed, prescribed and dispensed pills or medicines all in one go. They were not handed small pieces of paper covered with an illegible Latin scrawl and imperiously instructed to 'get this made up at the apothecary's.' Nor did the fact that Mr. Frost was only in the region of five and twenty detract from his qualifications. He had the knack of making people feel safe, and was never mysterious about their ailments. He told you straight out what he thought was wrong with you, unlike the late and unlamented Dr. Anderson, who wrapped up his diagnoses in unintelligible and terrifying language and frightened you half to death.

Amelia, though she would not have admitted it to a living soul, felt more than a passing interest in the young man. He was so very personable and clean-looking, and when he took off the white apron which he wore in the shop he might well have been mistaken for a gentleman. His hair was dark and wavy, so thick that he never saw the necessity of wearing a wig. His eyes were large, brown and very kind in expression, and when he smiled the perfection of his teeth was quite astonishing. It was those teeth, so white and dazzling, and the pleasing appearance of his long, slender and competent hands that had captured the heart of Amelia Darker.

As she entered the shop, causing the little brass bell to jangle its warning, and stood to survey the intriguingly neat rows of glass jars and bottles filled with every possible panacea known to mankind, Amelia was only too uncomfortably aware that her heart was beating more rapidly than usual.

Mr. Robert Frost came out from behind a wooden, box-like contraption pierced with a square pane of glass. His smile was not in the least like the smile of most of his breed. There was nothing in the least servile or ingratiating about it. It was merely charming and flatteringly interested.

'Miss Darker, good morning to you. What can I do for you today?'

'Good morning, Mr. Frost.' Eyes downcast because his gaze was a little too intent, a little too penetrating. 'I was wondering,' she began hesitantly '... I ...' She broke off, floundering helplessly, her gloved hands fidgeting with her reticule.

Gently, he prompted her. 'Some new medicament, perhaps, which you have but lately seen advertised in the London sheets?'

'Arsenic!' she blurted, immediately embarrassed by the drama inherent in the demand for a poisonous substance, then, before he could say anything else, 'I have heard that it whitens the complexion.' She put up a hand to cover the mark on her cheek and looked up at him appealingly, just in time to catch the swift comprehension and the humiliating, unmistakable signs of pity. She wished most fervently that she had not come, because he must think her silly and vain, which she undoubtedly was, and perhaps even wicked to despise the handiwork of the Almighty.

Palms flat on the counter-top he leaned

towards her, speaking earnestly. 'Miss Darker, it would be most unethical of me to recommend the application of so dangerous a substance to your complexion, which is exceedingly delicate and fair, if you will permit me to say so. I can see that you are troubled by the birth mark upon your face, and it may be that I can provide you with a less harmful preparation, to be rubbed in before an application of orris-root powder.'

She was looking at him with a mixture of wonder and gratitude. 'You are the first person, Mr. Frost, who has ever applied the correct term to the mark upon my face. Always it is "poor Amelia's affliction," or "Amelia's misfortune," or even "Amelia's *visitation*," but never, I fear, "the birth-mark on Amelia's face."'

His smile was open and frank as he told her, 'I am a firm believer in examining everything in the clear light of day, Miss Darker. Do not shy away from physical imperfections, I beg you. There are so few of us without them. If you will permit me?' His hand grasped her jaw, quite firmly, sending a tingle of excitement through her body. He examined her cheek with professional concern and at length pronounced judgement. 'It is not so dark as some I have seen and certainly, though I cannot absolutely guarantee that my preparation will totally conceal the mark, it will do much to nullify its effect upon the observer.'

She almost wept with relief. 'I cannot think why I did not ask you before, Mr. Frost.'

He said, 'I think perhaps, Miss Darker, that you had convinced yourself that nothing could be done. One's family are rarely helpful over such things I am afraid.' His smile was mischievous. 'May I ask what prompted this sudden access of vanity?'

The way he said it the remark sounded pleasant and gently teasing. Thus might her brother James have spoken to her. She hesitated briefly, knowing that her family would think it shocking of her to confide in a tradesman, for as such Mr. Frost was regarded. The need to tell someone got the better of her instincts for discretion, however, and she answered soberly, 'Papa told me this morning that I am to marry Sir Edward Mulliner, and that I *must* take him, for I shall never get another gentleman to offer for me.'

She glanced down at her feet. 'There is my leg too, you see, and you have no magic potion for that.'

He replied quietly, 'Neither is there any magic potion which could have made you the most charming and intelligent young lady it has ever been my good fortune to meet. Has it not occurred to you, Miss Darker, that what you regard as your deficiencies are barely noticeable to those who truly admire you?'

She blushed, and now the reticule was

undergoing very severe torment indeed. He added, 'I find it very hard to believe that Sir Edward Mulliner will be your only suitor, Miss Darker.'

'Papa thinks so, and so do Gussie and Sarah, though they would never be so heartless as to say so.'

'Well, I do *not!*' Robert Frost made this statement so vehemently that Amelia stared at him in surprise, and read in his features something which she had never thought possible. 'Oh, sir! You are always so kind!'

'Not kind, Miss Darker.' Boldly, he picked up one of her gloved hands and held it between his own as though it were a very precious object indeed. 'Extremely selfish and conceited to nurture a hope that you might return the regard I have for you.'

'But I *do!*' she countered artlessly, and with equal earnestness, and then blushed again at her own forwardness.

His gaze had become quite astonishingly fierce. 'Would your father consider . . . ? Can it be possible that . . . ?'

Sadly, she shook her head, distressed that she must, however tactfully, remind him of his inferior status.

'No,' he agreed ruefully. 'It was quite wrong of me to declare myself like that. Can you ever forgive me, Miss Darker?'

'For what, sir?' Her tone was as ardent as his look. 'For the suggestion that you should become my suitor? There is nothing to forgive.'

She leaned towards him, so close that he could smell the sweet scent of the lavender water which she had sprinkled on her bodice. 'Do you not think, Mr. Frost, that we should fight for the right to choose our own partners in life? Should we not endeavour to attain the unattainable?'

His eyes widened in disbelief, then he laughed delightedly. 'For my part, nothing would please me better!'

She spoke urgently now, carried away by her own daring, and at the same time afraid that someone would enter the shop before their conversation could be concluded. 'I may not marry until the period of mourning for dear Mama is over, and by that time, please God, my brother James will have returned. If anyone can persuade Papa it is he. James is clever with words and may be able to think of some argument which will carry enough weight to ensure a happy outcome.'

A slight frown creased his forehead. 'Are you so sure then that Mr. James Darker will approve of me as a suitor for your hand?'

Amelia bit her lip. She was not at all sure, but the dream she had manufactured during the last quarter of an hour must be allowed to go on, so that the nightmare might be squeezed out and for the moment disregarded. In any case, she told herself, dreams did sometimes come true. Seeing the increasing look of doubt

91

in the eyes of the apothecary she burst out, 'We can at least try!'

To her immense relief pleasure visited his face again. 'You may depend upon me for that, Miss Darker, but I would not have you anger your father on my account.' He placed one hand on his head in a totally boyish gesture. 'Miss Darker, you have turned my day into a holiday. I feel like shutting up my premises for the whole day and going to dance a hornpipe on the village green.'

She giggled excitedly. 'That, I fear, would be most imprudent and would completely destroy the good reputation you have been at such pains to build up. If we are to succeed in our dangerous enterprise we must proceed with great circumspection. Oh, heavens!' She giggled again. 'I really feel quite fraudulent. It was my vanity which led me here, and instead of being punished I have been rewarded with the knowledge that I am not wholly repugnant to the opposite sex. Sir, you have quite restored my confidence in myself.' Her shining face testified to the truth of these words. 'At least I shall always be able to find an excuse for coming to see you. You will be quite astonished at the number of minor ailments which will attack me until James comes home.' Keep up the dream, Amelia. It is so very much better than the reality.

'And you at the number of times my errand-boy is taken sick and I must deliver personally anything that is required up at Frinton Park.'

When Amelia Darker had taken her leave the apothecary fell into positive transports of delight as he pictured the little house he would soon be able to afford to buy should he decide to take a wife. William Darker was bound to be generous over the matter of his eldest daughter's dowry. He might soon be able to open a bigger and better establishment in Brighthelmstone or Lewes. Brighthelmstone would be the better place, he thought, because there he might be lucky enough to be patronised by royalty. For Robert Frost too the dream was bright, the only difference being that in his case he really thought it could come true.

*   *   *

Sir Edward Mulliner carefully lowered his ponderous bulk into a comfortable leather chair which William had introduced into the saloon for his own personal comfort, and stared across at his intended who was nervously dispensing tea. To Amelia's horror Papa had arranged for her to take tea alone with Sir Edward, and had banished her sisters to the schoolroom and the ignominy of nursery tea.

'You will converse with Sir Edward for one half hour,' William had instructed, 'after which you will ring the bell for Elise to take away the tray. That will also be the signal for me to come and join you.' This plan of campaign was relayed by William with eyes averted from his daughter's face, for he was quite unable to meet the look of direct accusation continually bent upon him. The feelings of guilt which Amelia aroused in him were accompanied by extreme irritation at her failure to appreciate the effort he was making on her behalf. God save him from vapourish females!

Amelia slopped a little of the tea in the saucer as she passed the cup across to Sir Edward, and was not reassured by the knowing smile which spread itself over his plump, swarthy features. In an age when men did not favour beards Sir Edward looked as though he had one waiting to spring out at any moment. His valet shaved him once a day, which Sir Edward considered sufficient, but by four o'clock each afternoon the shadow on his chin had become markedly pronounced. His face was large and heavy, in keeping with his body. Once, when in London, he had gone to Lloyd's Coffee House and had come under the penetrating scrutiny of Mr. James Gillray, the famous cartoonist. Mr. Gillray had declared it a crying shame that Sir Edward was not in public life, since his face was a caricaturist's dream. 'You've a hint of savagery about the mouth, sir,' Mr. Gillray had informed him with his usual disregard for courtesy. 'I'd like to put that face on the body of a scorpion!'

Amelia was unaware of Mr. Gillray's opinion of her suitor. Nevertheless, she thought him monstrous ugly, though unlike the cartoonist, she was not concerned with the subtleties lurking in the quirk of a lip or the flare of a nostril.

Sir Edward took the offered cup and heaving himself up from the depths of the chair re-deposited his bulging posterior on the sofa beside Amelia. 'What a touchy little thing you are,' he observed, noticing how she recoiled at his proximity. 'Like an over-bred mare,' he went on. 'You are not afraid of me, are you?'

He had a high-pitched, rather effeminate voice, completely at variance with his physical appearance. She found the voice as repulsive as the face. His question having elicited no reply he persisted, 'Well, miss, are you?'

Amelia took a large swallow of tea by way of fortifying herself and murmured, 'No, indeed, sir. We are quite tolerably well acquainted I think.'

'And shall be better in due course, eh?'

'Perhaps.'

A slight cloud darkened Sir Edward's brow. 'Your Papa has told you exactly what is proposed, has he not?'

'Of course.' Her distant manner caused the frown to deepen. 'Yes, well, I wondered. Your demeanour, my dear, is not that of a lady who is taking tea with her future husband.'

She felt rebuked and longed to say something clever and rebuffing, as Aunt Sophie would have done. After what seemed an interminable pause she managed, 'Papa only told me this morning. I have not yet had time to get used to the idea that I am to be married.'

'No, I suppose you ain't.' His eyes wandered to her leg. 'Thought to fetch up an old maid I shouldn't wonder.'

Her leg stung as though he had kicked it. A downward glance assured her that the hem of her blue silk gown completely hid the special shoe which Papa had had made for her in Lewes. His eyes were now exploring the rest of her figure, rather like a dealer examining a cracked piece of porcelain which, solely by virtue of its rarity, still retains a certain intrinsic value. They finally came to rest upon her lace-trimmed bodice, which she wore quite low in the fashion of the day, and the smile was back again on his lips. She had well-rounded breasts, pushed up by her boned stays. He was afforded a tantalising glimpse of creamy-smooth skin beneath the gathered flounces of lace. Sir Edward swallowed his tea in a single gulp, set aside his tea-cup, and moved a little closer to Amelia. Quickly she leaned forward to pour him another cup, but he forestalled her by taking the teapot out of her hand and depositing it with a clatter on the tray. He edged even nearer, and one arm went about her waist. The other hand toyed with the ribbons on her bodice.

'Please, Sir Edward!' She was outraged and very very frightened. She struggled to free herself, but his grip about her waist was like steel and the fingers at her bodice began to claw and tug until her right breast was almost completely exposed. Holding back a scream, for it would be unthinkable for a third party to bear witness to her humiliation, she began to reproach her ardent suitor. 'Sir, you quite forget yourself. I am no whore that you should use me so. Were my father to learn of your behaviour he would challenge you to a duel.'

The grip about her waist did not slacken and he began to laugh, very softly. 'Your Papa, my dear Amelia, fears that you may do something foolish rather than marry a man as old as myself. You have a mind of your own he tells me. Well, that is all to the good. It makes the chase more exciting, and you will not be the first nor the last wayward chit who is drilled to obedience by her future spouse. What I am trying to say, my dear, is that your Papa will not mind too much if you are somewhat ... er, for want of a better word, compromised.

'Of course, he urged me to be discreet ... and I shall ... if you are kind to me, for I know only too well that an incautious word in the ears of the ladies would mean your total ostracism from every function in the county. Come now, give me your lips, and that shall suffice for the

97

present.'

Suddenly, Amelia's sturdy, independent spirit reasserted itself. Everything was crystal clear to her now. Papa had secretly connived at the ruin of her reputation in the hope that she would be grateful to marry this old lecher. Indeed, she would have no choice but to marry him. Tearing herself free from the obnoxious embrace she seized the bell and rang it furiously.

'You jade!' he panted. 'You shall pay for that, miss.'

Reluctantly he relinquished his hold on her, just in time, for Elise knocked on the door of the saloon and came in to take away the tray, loaded with its silver and porcelain implements. The girl was followed a minute or two later by William, who exuded an air of false joviality which increased if anything his daughter's anger. She would make both Papa and Sir Edward feel excessively foolish.

'Papa!' she blurted, before William had a chance to sit down, 'did you give Sir Edward permission to ravish me?'

It was the last thing William had expected. His face took on the deep purplish hue of mortification and he bridled indignantly. 'What a preposterous thing to say to your own father! You will apologise at once, miss.'

Amelia ignored the counter-attack and persisted, 'Did you, Papa? Because if so, I must declare, here and now, that I find the thought extremely disagreeable, as would any well brought-up young lady.' She stamped her foot to give emphasis to her next words. 'I declare, I shall *not* be forced into marriage by such means!'

Like two guilty schoolboys the men exchanged glances, but William refused to be daunted by such a missish trick. He thought of Clarissa, and an acute sense of loss took possession of him. She would have known how to deal with a situation like this. Had Clarissa been alive the 'situation' would never have arisen in the first place. Clarissa would have schooled Amelia into accepting her fate, and would have informed her as to what to expect before and after she climbed into the marriage bed. Not all gentlemen were as forbearing as he had been in the months before his marriage. Some wanted a taste of the fruits to come, and who could blame them? In Sir Edward's case there was not a great deal of time left in which to enjoy the pleasures of the flesh. William said aloud—and firmly he hoped—'When couples are courting, it is customary for them to embrace now and then and to exchange kisses.'

'Quite so.' Sir Edward nodded agreement and regarded Amelia with a look of righteous indignation. Faced with this joint barrage of accusing stares Amelia did something quite out of character. She burst into tears.

'There, there!' Sir Edward patted her shoulder with a carefully avuncular caress.

'From now on, Amelia, I shall respect your delicacy of feeling, though it is hard for a man of my virility to keep my hands off a little chick like you.'

This in front of Papa, who seemed not in the least put out by the creature's insolence. Amelia longed to smash her fist into those blue, rapidly rotating orbs, which kept finding their way to her bodice. They have trapped me, she told herself. Please God, send James home in time to put a stop to their wickedness. The dream was no longer as believable as it once had been.

SEPTEMBER, 1790

Letter from James Darker to Mr. William Darker of Frinton Park in the County of Sussex, England

'Dear Papa,

'We left Paris on the seventeenth day of June, after a very enjoyable stay, and moved on to the town of Montpellier, which is as far west as we shall go I think. The town is renowned as a health resort and has a famous medical faculty specialising in herbal remedies. A great many English people are to be seen there, presumably in search of a cure. Hordes of apothecaries live in the town, and one may not walk more than ten yards without coming upon one of their establishments, which are not at all like our English ones. Mr. Frost's shop is a miracle of neatness and cleanliness by comparison. Many of the shops do not have fronts, and resemble nothing so much as market stalls, with pills and powders all jumbled together in horrid confusion.

'I was astonished to observe a gentleman stop at one of these places, poke about among the wares with his stick, and having finally decided which medicament took his fancy, sample it with an air of a connoisseur tasting a fine wine. So far as I could see he had not the least idea what remedy the medicine was to provide for what particular disease, for he barely glanced at the label and went on his way looking remarkably complacent for one who may have inadvertently poisoned himself!

'Lord Frederick, who by the way, is in excellent health and spirits, declared himself mighty relieved to depart from this town of ailing people, and even Mr. Brookes, who is not averse to trying all the latest remedies for rheumatism, from which he suffers most cruelly, remarked that he preferred to choose from one or two rather than to scramble his brains trifling with three or four hundred.

'Having left Montpellier, we decided to

take the Grenoble route through the Swiss Alps, since it provided us with an opportunity to visit the monastery of the Grande Chartreuse. Poor Mr. Brookes had not bargained for the lofty situation of this house of Carthusian monks, whose way of life is so excessively austere that one may only marvel how it is that they manage to live so long. Some of them, we were informed, are almost eighty years old and this on a diet of coarse fish, goats' milk cheese and fruit. Their guests, I am happy to report, fare better. We were given a dish of excellent creamed chicken, a very fine cheese, and some of their famous white wine which is a pale greenish-gold in colour and exquisitely dry.

'In the refectory where we took our repast there is a curiously wrought fountain which plays all the time, casting its water into a large porphyry shell. Mr. Brookes gallantly swore that our visit was well worth the effort of negotiating "those dreadful slippery steps hewn out of the side of the mountain." He declared that the roar of the waterfall made his head ache and the smell of pines affected the membranes in his nose.

'As we proceeded on our journey the scenery became yet more savage. Across the border of Savoy the mountains look almost perpendicular, with not a foothold to be discerned, the ledges going up in gigantic "steps," some higher than twelve feet. Torrents of water pour down the ledges, foaming and white like soap-suds, and the noise is quite deafening. Parson Ellsworthy would have no great difficulty in persuading his dilatory flock of the existence of God if he could but show them the Savoyard countryside. It convinces one, without the help of other, more esoteric arguments.

'The Savoyard peasants are ragged and dirty, a condition which they endeavour to hide beneath brightly coloured, lavishly embroidered clothes. It is a strange fact that many of them suffer from protuberances of the neck. These are huge round swellings which they actually regard as a sign of beauty. They decorate them with trinkets. I would be interested to have Mr. Frost's opinion upon the nature of this phenomenon. Perhaps you could ask him? The condition has no name, so far as I know, and does not seem to reduce their spirits in any way. Indeed, they are exceedingly lively.

'We reached Geneva on the tenth day of July and stayed there for two days, finding the people friendly and hospitable, though prices were high, it being commonly supposed that all Englishmen are wealthy. Lord Frederick says that this misconception has come about because the English are extravagant in an exhibitionist sort of way and lead the Genevans on to believe that

103

they have plenty of money. Therefore, it is their own fault that they pay dearly for everything.

'From Geneva we went on to Lausanne, which we all thought dirty and unattractive. The streets are very steep and Mr. Brookes very quickly complained of want of breath. We took pity on him and did not stay long. Berne was our next stop. It a very beautiful mediaeval city. The streets are wide, regularly built, and all the main shopping streets are lined with low vaulted roofs, extending over the pavement and supported by pillars. This means that the ladies can stand and stare into the windows even on the rainiest of days.

'The streets in Berne are kept clean by the criminals, who drag carts through the streets every morning, sweeping up all the rubbish they can find, and even with small brooms dusting all the public gates and iron railings. We thought they were lunatics run loose until someone explained the purpose of these extraordinary manœuvres. There is little to do in Berne after dark. Indeed, all over Switzerland it is quite common for the gates of towns to be closed as early as five o'clock in the afternoon. Drummers march along the ramparts of the town walls calling the people home. They have only just repealed the Sumptuary laws, and certain classes of person are forbidden to keep carriages. Parson Ellsworthy would not be able to drive his famous red and yellow phaeton here!

'It was now borne in upon us that the fearful necessity of crossing the Alpine passes into Italy could not be shirked. We decided to take the route through the Lanslebourg and Susa over Mont Cenis. At Lanslebourg our coach was dismantled and packed in its separate pieces on the backs of mules—a very singular performance—and we were persuaded to put on bearskins and fur hats against the cold. We then took our places in a kind of straw sedan chair fitted with long poles which the porters placed on their shoulders as they conveyed us along the path. The chair of this odd contrivance had no floor, which was exceeding disagreeable, for when the porters put it down to rest a while one was left sitting on the damp ground clutching for warmth a rapidly cooling hot-brick. Even the steady-footed mules constantly slipped and fell.

'At Lanslebourg there are two inns, both scarcely habitable. We chose one—in desperation—and discovered that it had no sitting-room, except that which served in common for postilions, porters, gentlemen, poultry and assorted hogs and goats. Damp sheets, black bread, brackish water, tough poultry and a smell of farmyard manure were our lot. All this we endured, we hardy band of Britishers, and were rewarded at last by a sight of the Italian lakes and the Plain of Lombardy, whose gentleness and fertility beggars description. The air was sweet and temperate and the vineyards all green. On the banks of the river ranges of white buildings with courts and awnings give shade to peasants making silk. Italians cultivate vines by planting them against fruit trees and posts, and allowing them to twine almost naturally from one to the other.

'We soon found that to travel through Italy in comfort it was necessary to hand out *douceurs* at every available opportunity. If a man told one the way he would expect a tip. One can tip a porter and then be asked for more, simply because the fellow has carried more than five pieces of luggage. The need to change money is, perhaps, the most infuriating thing of all. In Venice alone one is faced with the task of mastering the worth of lire, soldi, louis d'ors, sequins, ducatoons, testoons, julios, three sorts of pistole, four sorts of ducat and a variety of others. Having only just learned the difference between the sequin, the scudo and the livre, you may imagine our confusion. It was easy to fall prey to grasping inn-keepers, but Lord Frederick was not averse to bargaining for a fair price to avoid, as he said, being labelled a *minchione*, which is a ninny in our language.

'We visited Genoa, but were advised not to stay there too long. The city is full of beggars who importuned us constantly. The enjoyment one experiences when visiting the harbour is overcast by the evil-looking hulks in which Turkish prisoners are kept locked up in tiny cages. They scarcely have room to breathe. All the Genoan nobles and their wives attire themselves in black. A lady may only wear white in the first year of her marriage.

'From Genoa we went on to Florence, which is a town admired by all. It is situated in a circle of surrounding heights on which the white villas, olive groves and vineyards sparkle in the sunlight. It is a city planted in a garden. There are many things to do in Florence. One can go to buy wine from one of the palaces of the nobles, who advertise themselves as vintners by hanging bottles from their windows or gates, or one may take a night-time stroll in the Boboli gardens, where cypress and ilex cast long shadows in the moonlight across the crumbling statues. It is an eerie sight.

'We visited the mausoleum of the Medici family in the chapel of St. Lawrence, where the walls are of jasper, agate, touchstone, lapis lazuli and alabaster. The tombs of the great dukes are made of marble and oriental granite topped with jasper "pillows" enriched with jewels and ducal crowns. In the Corso we watched a horse race, although this seemed to us to be a very barbarous affair. The poor beasts are ridden hard, and there are nails placed under the saddles to irritate the animals and promote a faster speed.

'We also saw the paintings in the Pitti Palace and the treasures of the Uffizi, so many that they are impossible to describe in a letter. I have made a note of many which I will show you on my return.

'Milan was our next stop, and here Mr. Brookes was in his element. I must own that the paintings which he so admired in the Palazzo Brera must be among the finest in the whole world. Titians, Raphaels, Leonardos, Caraccis, Gallitias, Bassanos line the walls, and every possible subject is depicted. An amusing incident occurred when we visited the Palazzo. Some of the works of art are not considered fit for the eyes of young girls—according to the Italian mamas that is—and one formidable lady spent the entire morning shepherding her daughter around with one hand firmly attached to the poor creature's eyes, only removing it before a still life or a landscape, and clamping it back as they moved on in case the next picture showed carelessly exposed male genitals! Lord Frederick managed to wink at the little signorina between coverings and uncoverings, and was rewarded with the sweetest of smiles and a roguish tilt of the head. Fortunately Mama was engaged in conversation with another lady when this exchange took place.

'Milan cathedral, begun in 1536, is not yet completed. It is built of white polished marble, both inside and out. One chapel is in pure silver, all the panels carved and representing different stages in the life of St. Catherine, to whom it is dedicated. Veiled before the altar is an original relic of the saint's tooth, set in diamonds, and framed in gold and mother-of-pearl. Outside the cathedral we were all three accosted by pimps who offered us women of whatever colour and country we should desire.

'From Milan we went on to Venice, arriving there in the early morning to find the canals covered with rafts and barges filled with fruit and vegetables; loads of grapes, peaches and melons with crowds of purchasers hurrying from boat to boat. Noble Venetians come in from their casinos at this hour and meet to refresh themselves with fruit before they retire to sleep for the day. The nobles seem to spend most of the day in bed, or half asleep in a gondola. Their nights are passed either in gambling, or in the pursuit of some intrigue, while their wives remain at home. We saw St. Mark's. The arrangement of the buildings around the square is very fine. The Doge's residence and the tall columns at the entrance, together with the arcades of the public library, the lofty Campanile, and the cupolas of the ducal church, form a very striking group of buildings. There are many graceful buildings along the Grand Canal, the Ponte di Rialto, the church of Santa Maria della Salute, Santa Lucia and San Giorgio Maggiore.

'Lord Frederick and I were of the opinion that the people in Venice were more intriguing than the buildings. We saw the Doge, clad in purple silk trimmed with ermine, and a cloak of cloth-of-gold. His hat is tall and horn-shaped and on his feet he wears gold-painted sandals. Noblemen walk about in silk and fur-lined, ankle-length togas coloured black, red, cream or violet, according to their rank, and the ladies of the court have painted faces almost hidden behind veils. They cover their hair with blonde wigs.

'There are all sorts of entertainers in the street—oriental rope-dancers, jugglers, fortune-tellers and magicians in St. Mark's. After Venice we visited Padua and Bologna and then travelled over the Apennines to Rome, where we are presently residing, and shall stay for at least two months I think. We have already done some sight-seeing here, although we arrived but a week ago. It is a marvellous place, with many, quite singular features. The shops here, unlike those in London, do not bear the name of the proprietor over the door or window. Instead, everything goes by symbols. A cardinal's red hat denotes a tailor, a man smoking a pipe, a tobacconist, a bleeding arm or foot, a surgeon, and if you see a Swiss in the uniform of the papal guard, there you may find a lace merchant. At one particular barber's shop near the famous Villa Borghese there is a notice over the door which reads, "Here we castrate the singers in the papal chapels." The shops and stalls of a particular trade are all grouped together in one area. Cabinetmakers are to be found between Via Arenula and Piazza Campitelli, the watchmakers in Piazza Capranica and the booksellers around the Chiesa Nuova.

'The usual superstitions abound. We made a tour of the convent of the Capuchins and were shown "A cross made by the Devil", "A painting by St. Luke", and the subterranean cemetery whose galleries are filled with skeletons. Poor Mr. Brookes was sick.

'The Marchese di Ludovici, in whose house in the Piazza Barbaroni we are comfortably domiciled, is a very fine gentleman indeed. He is immensely hospitable and has a son and two very beautiful daughters. One of the daughters, the youngest, is destined to go into a convent. We are invited to see the ceremony of her veiling, which takes place in two weeks' time. Lord Frederick says it is a shameful waste of womanhood, especially since he is sure that Gabriella—that is her name—has no vocation.

'I hope, dear Papa, that everyone at home is well. Please to tell Amelia that I have found her a delightful model of the basilica of St. Peter. I know that she greatly admired the one belonging to Uncle Briggs-Watson. I believe he purchased his in Florence.

'I will write again after we move on. I hope my previous letters arrived safely. 'Your affectionate son, James Darker.'

'Dated this seventh day of September, 1790.'

Letter from Lord Frederick Oliver to his father, Charles Oliver, Earl of Adur.

'Dear Papa,

'Here we are in Rome, in the house of the Marchese di Ludovici. What an austere old body he is. Very stiff and formal. His wife and daughters are terrified of him. You did not warn me that he was such a martinet. I thank God, Papa, that I was born in England, where parents actually love their children, even if they do beat them occasionally.

'By the way, it was utterly inspired of you

to suggest James Darker as my travelling companion. He is a dear, good-natured fellow, and I hope and believe that we shall always be firm friends. Mr. Brookes is passing well, and is of the opinion that the climate of Italy is very favourable to his rheumatism. I should be greatly obliged, Papa, if you could arrange for a draft of £600 to be sent to the Bank of Boboli here in Rome. We have not, I think, been extravagant in our spending, but we shall need that amount if we are to proceed with and complete Mr. Brookes's itinerary.

'I am sorry that there is nothing much of interest to report, for which, honoured father, you should be mighty grateful, since it clearly points to the fact that we have been behaving impeccably, James and me. Please give my dearest love to Mama, and say that I have not forgot to purchase her gold lace, which she particularly requested me to do.

'Your affectionate and very devoted son,

Frederick Oliver.'
'Dated this seventh day of September, 1790.'

113

SEPTEMBER, 1790

Love at the Villa Ludovici

It took some careful, not to say stealthy
contriving, to meet her alone, but he managed
it on a stiflingly hot afternoon in September
during the hour of siesta. She too was breaking
the rules, and in her rebellion lay his chance of
success. The Marchese, secure in the
knowledge that his word was law, could never
have imagined that one of his daughters was in
such distress of mind that even the threat of his
icy displeasure could not deter her from taking
advantage of the only hour of solitude she was
likely to have during the enervating,
interminable day.

When she should have been sleeping,
therefore, in her cool, curtained chamber, with
its solid gold crucifix and life-sized statue of the
Holy Virgin, carved for her by Messire Bellini
himself, staring at her from a wall-niche, she
was walking among the lemon trees and the
dark, brooding ilexes which lined the paved
walks of the garden, and communing with the
classical statuary which had been carefully
copied from those unearthed in the ruins of
Pompeii.

Lord Frederick came upon Gabriella di
Ludovici in the sunken garden standing beside

a small, tinkling fountain whose clear water gushed forth from the mouth of a dolphin. His approach was cautious, for there was a nervous, shy quality about her which reminded him of the does in his father's park at home. Despite his care, the sound of his footfalls startled her, and she looked round fearfully as he stepped down into the little enclosed square which surrounded the fountain. A faint gasp of relief rewarded his temerity in thus seeking her out.

'Lord Frederick!' The sound of her high, lilting voice, with its delicious broken accent, went straight to his knees. He stammered most fearfully in reply, 'Signorina Ludovici, I c ... came b ... because I wanted to speak to you.'

'You should be taking your siesta,' she reproved, but with the merest hint of a smile.

'And should not you?'

She hung her head. 'Yes, but I cannot sleep, not even at night.'

He moved nearer to her and ventured, 'There is something troubling you perhaps, Signorina?' How very lovely she was. Her hair was raven's wing dark with a bluish glint to it, her eyes deep brown, almost black, and her pale complexion lacked the somewhat swarthy cast common among Italian women generally. Her true beauty, however, lay in the perfect composure with which she faced the world, the serenity of her expression betokening an inner quietness of spirit which only the greatest

115

possible tragedy in her life could have disturbed. For the first time since he had come to the Villa Ludovici Fred saw agitation marring the calm nobility of her features. Gone was the look of a Provost Madonna, in its place the stare of a frightened child.

This young Englishman was the only person who had ever looked at her as if she were a real person, thought Gabriella. *Madre* looked at her critically, continually on the watch for some flaw, physical or mental, which might appear to spoil her own perfect creation. *Padre* looked at her proudly, possessively, as he would at one of his priceless paintings or a piece of fine silver. As for her sister and her elder brother, they both looked at her as if she were part of the unchanging scene, though lately she had sensed a subtle shift of emphasis from the mundane to the spiritual in their attitude towards her. Gabriella was destined to become a Bride of Christ and to spend the rest of her days in the silence of the cloister. From now on she must be approached with delicacy, if not with actual reverence.

Gabriella had always heard that English gentlemen were cold and unfeeling, and that their morals left much to be desired. She was sure now that that was a falsehood circulated by people who either did not know the true facts, or who were envious of the English way of life. She had learned a lot about the latter during the past three weeks at the evening *conversazione*. Lord Frederick was a great talker. Unlike his quiet friend, he did not seem in any way awed by her father. Of course, the other gentleman was not an aristocrat, which probably accounted for the difference.

Lord Frederick had asked if anything was troubling her. Could she tell him? Could she turn him into her father confessor? The real-life guardian of her soul was of little use when it came to untangling the tortured web of her feelings, the terrible confusion of doubts and fears which had begun to lay siege to her heart. When she had expressed serious misgivings about a vocation Monsignore Rietti had sternly admonished her, and had bade her stay up the night long, kneeling before her *scanno di preghiera*, praying that her soul might be purified and her will subdued into obedience. She had been frightened to persist in case Monsignore told her father. As every Roman Catholic knew, the secrets of the confessional were not always held to be inviolable.

Gabriella looked into the earnest face of the young man standing before her and decided to take a chance. Lord Frederick might be the only man outside her own family whom she would ever have the opportunity of speaking to again. 'Sir, I *am* greatly troubled,' she admitted. 'Perhaps you would be so kind as to listen to the thoughts in my head?'

A faint smile illuminated her features. 'I do not ask for your advice, since no advice, however good or well intentioned, can alter the course of my life, or change my destiny. I am indulging a purely selfish whim in asking you to hear me. I am behaving like the child who needs to be comforted.'

The slow, gentle way in which she pronounced these self-condemning words brought out in Fred all the old instincts of male protectiveness. He was the knight errant about to rescue the damsel in distress. Presuming to take her hand, he led her towards a small stone bench enveloped in trailing yellow roses, and begged her to sit down. She complied with this request, arranging the folds of her white silk gown so precisely that she might have been about to sit for her portrait. It was a particularity of conduct which did not surprise him. Since coming to Italy he had frequently observed that Italian women were at great pains to present a wholly impeccable appearance to the eyes of the world. Not a hair, not a frill, not a jewel must be out of place. It was as though, having the image of the Madonna constantly before their eyes, they must strive to emulate Our Lady of Sorrows in every way possible, while at the same time attracting the admiration of the predatory male who, even after the defilement of the marriage bed, required them to be the essence of purity.

Lord Frederick, an essentially shrewd young man, deplored this putting of women upon pedestals, for if one of them were to be so careless as to fall off, the result could be disastrous. Had he been with an English girl he would have taken her hand; as it was, he was careful to keep a distance of at least six inches between himself and Gabriella as he waited for her to speak. She forbore to do so for so long that he thought she might have changed her mind, but at last, with a little sigh, she began, 'I have recently become a prey to doubts about my vocation. I do not think that God wants me to live the life of a *religiosa*.'

It was on the tip of Fred's tongue to say, 'It is what *you* want, Gabriella, that matters,' but he knew that this was not the expected reply to make to one who had been brought up penned in by the iron bars of Catholicism. He said instead, 'Your father, I would guess, does not know of your doubts.'

'No.' Her hands, writhing together in her lap, gave expression to her anguish.

'Should he not be told?'

'Oh, no!' she replied swiftly. 'You see, Lord Frederick, my going into a convent has a very special, how do you say? significance for Padre. When he was younger he fought in a local skirmish against the French. He was very badly wounded, and having accepted the last rites of our church made a vow that if God saw fit to spare him he would deliver in due time one of his daughters to be a bride of Christ.' She made a small despairing gesture with her hand, as if

119

to point out the futility of her situation.

'And you are to be offered up as a sacrifice to God?'

Her large eyes widened as she turned to stare at him. 'My life, yes. Myself as a person, no. I have nothing to do with it.' Her eyes, bent so intently upon him, held a look of reproof. 'Our lives are not our own, Lord Frederick. They are given to us by God as a gift, but the gift is not irredeemable. It may be demanded back at any time and sometimes, as in my own case, God may require it of us before our souls have left our bodies.'

'But, Signorina, you said just now that you thought God did not require you to become a religious.'

She inclined her head. 'That is only my *conclusion*. I am not sure. How *can* I be sure? I have prayed and prayed for enlightenment and guidance, but He does not answer. Monsigore Rietti would say that God is angry with me for doubting and has turned away His face.'

Yes, Monsignore Rietti would, Fred thought bitterly. Monsignore Rietti is not willing to see the church cheated of your very handsome dowry, my poor Gabriella.

'Signorina . . . Gabriella,' he said urgently, 'if your heart tells you that it is wrong to go into a convent obey its dictates, for if you do not only wretchedness lies in store for you in the years that are to come. You will spend your life in constant rebellion against the chains that bind

120

you, fretting to be free. You will pray for humility, for the meekness to accept your lot with a cheerful heart, but it will not come. Believe me, it will not come.

'Your faith will wither and die inside you, and your spirit will become like a dried-out lemon because the tree that bears it has been starved of water. Then you will rail against fate, and you will curse the God that made you.'

Her hands came up in a pathetic appeal for him to stop. She was shaking her head at him, but he knew that the words he had spoken had found their echoes in her own heart. 'I asked you to listen, Lord Frederick,' she said tremulously, 'not to say things like that.'

'A thousand apologies, my sweet Gabriella,' and now he was bold enough to take her hand. It seemed to require a home, so agitated was it, fluttering like a bird who cannot find its nest. He held it firmly and went on, 'Let us put it another way, since what I have said does not please you. Had the choice been your own, would the prospect of a husband and children have delighted you?'

A light sprang up behind her mournful eyes and she whispered, 'Yes, oh yes,' adding hastily because she was ashamed of her weakness, 'but the choice is not mine.'

'Is it not? Forgive me, but I thought that God, in His wisdom, had created man to be the arbiter of his own fate. Have you ever asked yourself, Gabriella, whether God desires that others shall decide your fate for you? Did He not give you freedom of will, a gift which sets you above the level of the animals? Did He not give you a brain which shall determine how you shall exercise that freedom of will? Do you know, with perfect certainty, that God has invested your father with the power to decide your destiny?'

'The vow ...' she faltered.

'... was made by a man *in extremis*. Did your father know that his offering to God was accepted? Did he *know*, without a shadow of doubt?'

' "Honour thy father and thy mother, that thy days may be long in the land," ' she quoted softly.

'But you, Gabriella, have equated honour with blind obedience, and is not blind obedience a sin? By its very nature it deprives one of the power of thought.'

'Your Protestant doctrines,' she murmured with a gently mocking smile, 'how very convenient they are. They can be bent to provide the answer to almost any question.'

'I speak only what I believe,' he answered quietly. 'My Saviour is the same as yours. The Man of Galilee is universal, it is just that we interpret His teachings a little differently, we Protestants. Who are *you* to say that *we* are wrong?'

'My God is a stern and unforgiving God.'

'And mine a loving God, with pity in His heart for the poor weak creatures He has created and placed upon this earth.'

She stared at him for a long time before speaking again, and he sensed in her attitude a kindling of hope, like a tiny spring of pure water forcing its way upwards to wash away the mud of dogmatism and guilty despair.

At length she said, 'No argument, however forceful, would convince my father to release me from his vow, nor would my mother aid me in this. She is completely subservient to his will. If it were possible for me to summon up the courage to break the chains that bind me it would mean my banishment from my family for ever. Whatever course I take, there can be no turning back.'

He was quick to take advantage of the first sign that she might be persuaded to essay the great leap and free herself. 'Would it be so abhorrent to you to marry a poor, simple gentleman who is half mad with love for you?' He had not dared to hope that such an opportunity to declare himself would ever come his way. It had seemed to be beyond the realms of possibility. The rules were too strict, the barriers too impenetrable. Invisible bonds, forged by their conspiracy, drew her to him. The thought of a life, gay with company, albeit far away from her beloved Rome, was so seductive that she felt dizzy with excitement and desire. 'I am of the Catholic faith,' she said regretfully.

'And may hold fast to that faith, even in a land of heretics.'

She said with longing, 'I cannot see how it can be possible.'

His laugh was boyish. 'Neither can I, but if you will give me an hour or two I have no doubt that I shall be able to devise a means to accomplish it.' The laughter in his voice, disappeared, and he was suddenly deadly serious. 'Gabriella, I would give anything for you to become my wife and live with me in England, bearing my children, and making the ladies of the county green with envy because one with so much beauty has never before been seen in Sussex, but I must be sure that you will not have repinings, that you will not feel guilty.'

'I think perhaps God has sent you to me as an answer to my prayers,' she said quietly. 'You are the earthly messenger I have been waiting for, Lord Frederick.'

Let her believe it. Let her believe in the justification which her own willing mind had conjured up. The distant chiming of musical bells signalled the end of the siesta hour and she was alarmed again, fearful of discovery, wretched at the thought of parting from one who had offered her the key to freedom.

'Tomorrow,' he said quickly. 'Come here again tomorrow in the siesta hour. You will come?'

'Yes, yes!' Her eyes were wide and terrified. 'Go now, please, Lord Frederick.'

He had not the heart to protest at his abrupt dismissal. It would have been like smacking a hurt child. 'Tomorrow,' he repeated firmly, willing her not to weaken. Then he sped back to the beautiful white villa which was his beloved's fortress-prison.

*　　　*　　　*

'There is no doubt at all that you have taken leave of your senses,' said James, buttoning his frilled cuffs. 'The best course to be pursued is for Mr. Brookes and myself to take you back to Piddingfold in a strait-waistcoat and hand you over to his lordship.'

The two young men were dressing for dinner on the night following Fred's encounter with Gabriella in the sunken garden. Fred was certainly not himself. Gone was the gay, flippant manner to which James had grown so accustomed, in its place a kind of desperate intent. His face looked thinner than ever, the cheeks very flushed, and the candid blue eyes had mysteriously darkened, as if coloured by the force of his emotions. His hair, usually so elegantly waved and curled, was in some disarray.

'Nothing can be achieved in this life unless one is bold,' he told his friend. 'That is where you and I differ, James. You are all for caution, a positive martyr to the conventions, whilst I am inclined to bend a given situation to suit my own will, to exploit it to the full, and thus achieve my heart's desire.'

'It must be my humble origins,' commented James drily. 'You are an aristocrat, so of course you may be forgiven for acting rashly and abusing the hospitality of your father's friend.'

Fred's face fell. 'Dear fellow, I have offended you. Will you forgive me?'

James turned towards him, placing a hand on his shoulder. 'You? Offend me? Believe me, my very dear friend, that is not possible. I have never had a brother, but you have made up for the want of one, and I pray that our friendship may be long, transcending any minor disagreements between us. It is because I value our relationship so highly that I feel bound to protect you from the consequences of your own folly. Think, Fred. What you propose doing is frankly outrageous.

'If I take your meaning correctly, the plan is that you and Gabriella shall be married during the hour of siesta in the Protestant church, and afterwards you will confront the Marchese with a *fait accompli*, in the vain hope that he will bless your union and wish you long life and happiness. *I* say that he will challenge you to a duel, and that he will enter into the deadly contest with a fixed determination to kill you.'

'Not if I take care to consummate the

marriage before he is made aware of the situation.'

'What difference would that make?'

Fred's forehead, creased with anxiety, showed how unsure he was of the validity of his arguments. He answered, 'A defiled girl may not enter a convent here. The rules, so I am given to understand, are specific on that point, and if the possibility exists—as it must if consummation has taken place—that Gabriella is with child, what other course can the Marchese pursue than to agree to our marriage?'

'Which has already been solemnised in a church full of heretics who, a century ago, would have been burned at the stake!' James was quite angry now, an anger prompted more by fear than disapproval. He went on, 'They say that love is blind, and by heaven I believe it. You cannot see further than the end of your own nose.'

'Whatever you may say,' returned the other, 'I am determined to marry Gabriella. To have ventured and lost is better than never to have ventured at all.'

James made a noise of disgust. 'You are full of clichés today, Fred. They don't suit you.'

'Shall you help us?' The appeal was made with such directness and simplicity that James was touched. Previously it had always been he who had followed in the wake of his boisterous friend, sharing his often hilarious adventures, content to allow himself to be amused. The case was different now. Now it was Fred who depended upon him, in a matter so close to his heart that it would have been churlish to refuse to help him in every way possible.

James felt bound to add one final word of warning. 'The Marchese is a strange man, given to moods, and markedly lacking in humour. His daughters are his possessions. I have caught the peculiar brooding quality of his regard upon them, as if knowing one day that he must give them up, one in marriage, the other to God, he seeks to impress their images upon his mind so indelibly that he will never forget how they were before they left his house. They are like precious objects to him, outshining his son, whom one would expect him to value more highly. If you interfere with his plans for Gabriella, Fred, he may very well kill you, and Gabriella too. I imagine he will not be averse to making two sacrifices to God instead of one.'

Fred's smiling face was full of wonder. 'How very perceptive of you, dear fellow. You amaze me. You are right, of course, but the chance must still be taken.'

With a sigh James bowed to the inevitable. 'What do you want me to do?'

'Merely to wait in the sunken garden until our return. If anyone should chance to come into the garden while you are there, be good enough to make some excuse and walk through the garden door into the street to intercept us, so that we may wait until all is clear before entering the villa. We do not want a scene to take place outside its walls.'

'No, indeed,' agreed James grimly. 'The scene within will be enough to burst them asunder.' Struck by a sudden thought he asked, 'Is not a licence required here, in order that one may marry? Are not religious ceremonies in Italy attended by all sorts of formalities?'

'Procured, dear fellow,' replied Fred with something of a return to his old gaiety, 'and dated the seventeenth of this month. I had to give a false name for Gabriella, of course, as her father's name is so well known in the city, but that does not invalidate the legality of the ceremony.'

'Worse and worse!' moaned James, slapping his forehead with the palm of his hand. 'The seventeenth do you say? Is not that the day before Gabriella was to enter the convent? Cutting it a bit fine, ain't you?'

'There had to be a week's notice,' Fred explained. 'No banns to be called every Sunday for three weeks, or any of that nonsense.'

'How strange,' murmured his friend. 'I thought the rules of the Protestant church were universal, like those of the Church of Rome.'

Fred shrugged. 'Something to do with civil law I shouldn't wonder,' he offered vaguely. 'I asked not the reasons, dear fellow.'

The two were out in the white-walled

129

passage and about to descend the staircase to the lower floor when Fred, pausing at the head of the stairs, caught at James's sleeve and whispered urgently, 'Dear fellow, can I rely on you to see that no blame is attached to poor old Brookes if anything goes amiss? I should not want him to suffer on account of my rashness.'

'You have the grace to admit that what you are doing is rash then? You do surprise me ... *dear fellow*.'

Having failed to coax a smile from his friend's pale, sober countenance, James went on to promise, 'You may rely upon me. Our friend shall not suffer.'

Fred managed something like his customary grin. 'Spoken like an aristocrat, dear fellow.'

*   *   *

In contrast to the many elaborately furnished churches he had seen since the beginning of his stay in Rome, Fred found the plain austerity of the Protestant chapel in the Via Barbaroni refreshing. It reminded him of the village church at home, and he was seized by a sudden severe attack of longing for the sight of an English summer, part of whose charm was its unpredictability. Here the sun-scorched days, each like its predecessor, each presaging its successor, went on and one, seemingly for ever. The unchanging scene was enervating. Perhaps it accounted for the way in which everyone seemed to accept their fates, good or otherwise, as God-ordained. There were no sharp nips of wind or rain to prod them into rebellion.

With Gabriella on his arm and two witnesses, bribed into church off the street, following closely behind, Fred walked down the aisle towards a grey-haired man, robed in black vestments and with a band of white at his throat, who stood waiting for the bridal pair. As the man's lineaments came more sharply into focus Fred discerned upon them an expression of ineffable boredom. He almost laughed as it occurred to him that in Rome business must be pretty slow.

The ceremony took just five minutes to perform, after which the two newly-weds stole away from the church. Made apprehensive by the booming chimes of the church clock striking the half hour, they ran the five hundred yards back to the Villa Ludovici where they came upon the faithful James pacing up and down in the sunken garden and looking thoroughly wretched. The sight of the pair, hand in hand, and giving the appearance of going to their execution, which they well might be, did nothing to allay James's fears. The deed was done. Now it was almost time to pay the reckoning. All three crept quietly back to the villa, unaware of the observant and breathless watcher hidden among the ilexes.

Later that day Fred came to James's room and with an embarrassed reserve confessed

131

that he had consummated his marriage, hastening to add, 'I should not dream of burdening you, dear fellow, with such details, were it not for the fact that I may later need an ally.'

'What happens now?' James wanted to know, and suddenly wished he was anywhere else on earth.

Fred seemed even more embarrassed. 'Gabriella ... my wife ... is to spend the night in prayer in the family chapel. We intend to make an announcement early tomorrow morning before breakfast. That way we can catch everyone with an empty belly.' He laughed nervously. 'I for one can never arrange my thoughts in an orderly manner when I am hungry.'

James felt desperately sorry for his friend, who was now openly clutching at straws. 'Dinner would choke me tonight,' he confessed. 'I think I shall plead an indisposition.'

'No!' Fred sounded alarmed. 'Please ... dear fellow, you must come down. Everything should look normal, d'ye see?'

James gave in without a fight. 'Just as you say.'

'I shall never forget what you have done for me.'

'I have done precious little except keep a still tongue in my head.'

'Exactly what I meant, dear fellow.'

Tragedy at the Villa Ludovici

Taken from the Journal of James Darker, written on the twenty-fifth day of September, 1790.

*   *   *

'My dearest sister Amelia has often urged me to keep a journal. It enables one to get things in their proper perspective she is fond of repeating, and purges the soul. It is like a confessional. If ever I needed a confessor it is now. Thus, accepting Amelia's advice, which is never anything but sensible to the greatest degree, I intend to put down everything as it happened on the day of Lord Frederick Oliver's wedding to Signorina Gabriella di Ludovici.

'Whether I shall ever confide the events written down here to another living soul seems doubtful, because unless one has actually lived through an experience such as I am about to recount, one cannot even begin to grasp its essential nature, or endow the facts with any sort of credibility. But I must cease digressing, which is only my way of putting off the evil hour, and make a beginning.

'When we came down to dinner on that fateful night everything seemed so very much as usual that it was difficult to believe such a drastic upheaval had taken place in the circumstances of two of our number. I think I shall carry in my mind's eye a picture of that dining-room or *sala da pranzo* as the Italians call it, for as long as I draw breath. It was a long, narrow room, the focal points of which were the exquisite mosaic floor and the series of family portraits lining the walls. Like all the rooms in that magnificent villa the walls were painted white, to give an appearance of coolness, one supposes, and indeed when one steps down into the *sala da pranzo* one becomes immediately conscious that the temperature has dropped by at least five degrees which, though I am hazy about the mechanics of it, has something to do with the style of architecture.

'The windows are uncurtained, which is an extraordinary sight to an Englishman, and the furniture is in a style I have never seen before, being fashioned out of Italian rosewood and of an elegant simplicity which gives the lie to the assumption prevalent in England that 'foreigners have no taste.' The appurtenances of the dinner-table are always extremely elaborate, with quantities of curiously-wrought fine silver and cut-glass maintained in shining perfection by a positive army of servants. There is always a centre-piece of flowers, which seems to me an odd conceit, and also—a thing I have never seen before—a complementary, smaller arrangement beside each place-setting. I must say I find this very agreeable and am often caught out by the

134

Marchese applying my nose to my own particular little nosegay in order to inhale the heavy perfume of the flowers. By his expression I gather he thinks the habit eccentric.

'On the evening in question I took my place at table with a distinct feeling of unease, for never in my life have I seen two creatures look so positively guilty as Lord Frederick and Gabriella. During the course of the meal, when conversation was buzzing about the table—English being spoken in deference to Fred and myself—these two spoke very little, but with downcast looks and an air of enduring some very painful ordeal, stared at their plates, their appetites seemingly quite gone. What little they did eat was chewed and chewed, and swallowed so reluctantly that it was like watching people undergoing torture. To my very great relief none of the other members of the family appeared to notice anything at all unusual in their demeanour. The Marchesa was her usual graceful and charming self, sporting diamonds worth a king's ransom, and smiling in that gentle, forgiving way of hers. Why I should think her smile forgiving I cannot tell. It is just the way she looks at one after one has made some observation, as if to say, 'Sir, that is not an intelligent thing to say, but I excuse you because it is obvious to me that you know no better.'

'Katrina, the eldest daughter of the house, sat on my left and kept up a lively flow of chatter based on the sights Fred and I had seen in Rome, and the sights still remaining to be seen. Paolo, the Marchese's only son, made several, futile attempts to draw Lord Frederick into conversation and at length gave up with a small, puzzled but infinitely polite smile, turning his attention to a very stout lady wearing a black lace mantilla, who was seated on his right, and whose daughter he is to marry.

'As for the master of the house, I had never seen him more at ease. He even managed a smile now and then, often directing these thin travesties of good humour at me, who knew not how to receive them, so rarely was the dish served up. I own I am not at my best with the Marchese di Ludovici. He symbolises for me the true meaning of the word aristocrat, or am I confusing it with autocrat? Austere, highly intelligent, humourless and inflexible to a degree, he rules his household with the iron fist in the velvet glove, and though he is the soul of courtesy to me as his guest, I get the uneasy feeling that were I to do or say something which did not accord with his code of how a gentleman should behave I should find myself banished from his household in very short order. To say that he inspires fear in my breast is, perhaps, a little too exaggerated. Suffice it to say that he makes me nervous. He seems to sense this and goes out of his way to be kind to me, often deliberately drawing me into a conversation if he thinks I am allowing myself to be excluded.

'As I sat, munching delicious chunks of pineapple, and observing Fred with an anxiety which I fervently hoped was not betrayed by my countenance, the Marchese addressed me in his faultless English with: "Mr. Darker, shall you go further south after you leave Rome, or is it your intention to turn back now through Germany and the Low Countries?"

'The question evoked little fidgetings from Brookes, who would gladly have answered in my place, so obsessed was he with our itinerary. Since the question had been directed at me, however, and unhappily aware that the Marchese regarded him as an underling, and a heretical underling at that, Mr. Brookes wisely curbed his enthusiasm and took a sip of wine instead. I murmured something to the effect that we had thought of visiting Naples and the ruins at Pompeii.

'"Ah, yes," replied he. "You will be in disgrace with your fellow-countrymen if you do not visit Pompeii. It has been responsible for great innovations in English society. Mr. Josiah Wedgwood obtained his ideas for Etruscan-style pottery at Pompeii, and it has served as an inspiration for the furniture of Messrs. Sheraton and Hepplewhite."

'These familiar names on the lips of an Italian nobleman took me by surprise, and he must have sensed my astonishment for he remarked, "I was in England five years ago, Mr. Darker, and was quite impressed by the manner in which these gentlemen had adapted such interesting archaeological discoveries to improve their own designs."

'I asked him about Mount Vesuvius, at which he smiled and said that every tourist made the ascent of Vesuvius as a point of pride. "A saddle-horse will convey you to the top," he assured me, "or almost to the top. If you wish to proceed to the limit you must go on foot and take the risk of getting your clothes scorched. If you are really an intrepid traveller you may actually look down into the flaming bowl of the mountain and receive a foretaste of what it is like to spend eternity in hell."

'At this Brookes's face was a picture to behold, and I freely admit that the Marchese's words struck a chill to my own heart. I swear that it is not just with the advantage of hindsight that I thought them significant.

'After that the conversation touched upon such diverse subjects as wine-growing, bull-fighting and the oddities of the King and Queen of Naples, and it was not without some measure of relief that I saw the ladies depart for the *salone*. I could not bear the way Gabriella determinedly refused to look at Fred. The ugly suspicion began to grow in my mind that she now bitterly regretted her spur-of-the-moment decision to marry him, and was struggling with thoughts of purgatory and mortal sin.

'To the accompaniment of masculine small-talk the port was circulated several times, and we were about to rise from the table when the Marchese requested that we would be pleased to excuse him from bearing us company in the *salone*. Tomorrow, as we were aware, his younger daughter was to enter the Convent of the Sacred Heart to begin her novitiate. There were certain matters to arrange. We understood? We did, and together with the husband of the fat lady, and a gentleman of indeterminate age and station who had been introduced to us as the cousin of the Marchesa, we repaired to the upstairs *salone*.

'By this time Lord Frederick looked as though he was undergoing his own personal martyrdom, but he managed to struggle through the rest of the evening, partnering the Marchesa at several games of quinto and even succeeding in winning a little money.'

*   *   *

'Ten minutes past the hour of midnight sleep still eluded me, and the heat seemed intolerable. As I lay, tossing and turning in my bed and trying to find a cool place on the pillow on which to rest my burning cheek, I began to be assailed by strange notions. I suddenly felt vulnerable, clad only in my nightshirt, in this alien house, and the desire, at first firmly resisted, grew in me to rise and put on my clothes, even to pack my bags, for after the coming *dénouement* we should surely be on our way, wrenching Gabriella, unblessed and weeping, from the bosom of her family. The desire to be fully clad at length overcame the abuse I mentally heaped upon myself for being a coward, and I gave way to it. Not only that, but the chamber itself seemed to close in upon me and the impulse to depart from it was strong.

'What should I do? Wander in the garden till dawn, preparing myself for God knew what, or prowl about the villa like a ghost and take the chance that a wakeful servant would come upon me looking as furtive as a nocturnal thief? At length I bethought me to proceed to the gallery, which was situated on the first floor and which ran the entire length of the house from north to south.

'The west wall of the gallery had been pierced at intervals with cruciform apertures in order that those members of the household who were indisposed might look down into the chapel below and see the elevation of the Host at Mass. I had a vague, undefined notion that I wanted to observe Gabriella saying her prayers, keeping the night-long vigil which was required of her. At the same time it occurred to me that to play the *voyeur* was hardly the act of a gentleman. Nevertheless, I determined upon it, and am now convinced that something other than my own will directed my footsteps that night.

'Soft-footed, I crept along the passage leading from my chamber and turning left at the end, entered the gallery, which was furnished with the usual array of paintings, but boasted no furniture save a chair or two. It was strictly for indoor perambulation when the weather made it inadvisable to take a turn out of doors. No sound disturbed the utter stillness of the villa as I padded my way like a conspirator down the length of the gallery, making for the aperture which looked directly down upon the altar. A single torch, protected by a glass shade, illumined the darkness. As I reached the aperture and looked down I formed in my mind's eye an image of the scene which would be disclosed to view. Gabriella in white, her head veiled, kneeling in prayer before the altar, upon which huge white candles would be burning steadily in their silver sconces. Above the bowed head the sanctuary lamp, hanging by its silver chains, would give off its mysterious red glow.

'This calm and pleasant image was shattered in a moment, and a *tableau* met my eyes which caused me to gasp and recoil, so great was the shock I received. There, prostrated before the altar was the figure of a girl, naked from the waist up, and with her arms spread sideways in imitation of a cross. The bottom half of her body was swathed in coarse black serge, and her head had been shaved. Pools of black

141

surrounded her shorn head like a dark halo. That the figure was Gabriella's I could not doubt.

'Almost upon the same instant that I applied my face to the aperture a tall figure, robed in black—by its bulk I took it to be that of a man, though I could not be sure, for the head was cowled—began to belabour the girl's exposed back with a knotted scourge. The blows, rhythmically applied, produced no smallest sound from the victim. Horrified, I began to count, imagining in my ignorance that twelve strokes would mark the limit of the creature's barbarity. My mental barrier was soon passed, and now bright spots of blood began to appear on her flesh neatly aligned as the knots on the scourge found the same mark again and again. It was done with sickening expertise.

'Fifty of these brutish blows were delivered, and as I stared, fascinated at the awful spectacle before me, I saw, emerging from the shadows of the chapel the tall, thin figure of the Marchese di Ludovici, he who had spoken so glibly of our future travels at dinner but a few hours before. Beside him walked his wife. Together they stared down at the mutilated back of their younger, most beautiful daughter, and both made the sign of the cross with a devoutness which made me want to vomit. Worse things had been done in the name of Christianity, but hardly could they have been committed with such cold-blooded ardour. The figure with the scourge removed his cowl and I saw that my guess had been correct. It was a man, one whom I believed to be the family's confessor. I had seen him about the villa from time to time. Always he had ignored my presence, as though to speak to a heretic might in some way contaminate him. His head was tonsured and I believe he was of the Order of St. Benedict.

'At a signal from the priest two more figures stepped from the shadows. They were nuns. Bending down they raised Gabriella to an upright position and quickly clothed the upper half of her body with a white linen shift. She gave a small, agonised moan and her head fell to one side. One of the nuns slapped her face and she murmured something unintelligible. They turned her about to face her parents, forcing her to her knees as they did so. In a stern voice the priest bade her ask forgiveness for the terrible sin she had committed. Again she said something which my straining ears could not catch, and the Marchese nodded as though satisfied.

'The priest called her sharply by name. 'Gabriella!'

'Her face, deathly white in the light of the candles, was turned painfully towards him as he addressed her. "You have suffered but a part of the penalty for your most terrible sin. Tomorrow will begin the second part. After the ceremony of entering the novitiate is concluded you will be placed in a cell and will remain in solitary confinement for six months, until the purging of your soul can be accomplished. There you will drink the water of penitence and partake of the bread of humility, and you will spend the days and nights on your knees in prayer so that you may make atonement, purifying yourself, in order that you may be fit to take your place with your sisters in the convent.

' "You will wear upon your breast a placard bearing the words 'fornicator' and 'heretic', and this shall be held in place by means of an iron collar fastened about your neck. The collar shall be removed when your days of solitary confinement are over."

'Upon hearing this sentence Gabriella turned her head away and was led by the nuns up to the altar rail, where she was again pushed to her knees. On either side of her the nuns knelt too and began to chant prayers.

'The Marchese addressed the priest. "Our guests shall be told that Gabriella has taken her own life because she has committed a sin too terrible to live with. Then I shall request them to leave my house and abandon us to our grief." His next words were filled with as much venomous scorn as could be put into them. "Heretics! They will never understand our ways. May their black souls rot in hell for all eternity!"

'The Marchesa spoke for the first time. "If

144

she should prove to be with child ..." She faltered, and for a moment I thought that icy calm of hers would break, but she recovered herself quickly and repeated more firmly, "If she should prove to be with child, what is to be done?"

' "She will not be permitted to foul this earth with the blood of a heretic," came the monstrous reply. "She shall die first."

'I crept back to my chamber with a full and sorrowful heart. It occurred to me to wonder why Lord Frederick had not been as wakeful as I, and I took pause at his chamber door as I passed so that I might listen for signs of his stirring. I could hear nothing, and on an impulse I turned the handle of the door and tip-toed in. He was sound asleep, lying flat on his back and snoring. I thought this passing strange for one who had enough on his mind to banish sleep for ever. A small flicker of alarm ran through me. I leaned over him and inhaled the unmistakable odour of laudanum on his breath. So, he had been drugged! Carefully put out of action while their barbarous pagan rites took place in the chapel. Though bitterly angry I experienced at the same time a sense of relief that Lord Frederick had been spared the awful sight which it had been my lot to behold. It would have scattered his wits. Obviously the Marchese had not considered either Brookes or myself as a threat to his authority.

'My anger was occasioned by the fear that

they might inadvertently have over-dosed my poor, love-sick friend. Happily this was not the case. I wondered, not without a sinking sensation in the pit of my stomach, how Lord Frederick would react in the morning, faced with the consequences of his rash adventure. I went back to my room and laid me down on the bed, grateful that an enviable foreboding had made me dress and pack up my things.

*   *   *

'It had become customary for us in this hot climate to take a turn in the garden before breakfast. I thought Lord Frederick would be there as usual, impatiently awaiting his bride, and ready to take her back into the villa in order to announce the fact of their marriage. As I descended to the garden I mentally rehearsed what I should say to him. I resolved never to tell him what I had seen, and prayed earnestly that the Marchese would quickly break the news of Gabriella's supposed death, followed by a formal request for our immediate departure.

'Lord Frederick was, as I had imagined, pacing up and down, while Brookes, busy with his notebook, peered with the ardour of an obsessed botanist at the profusion of plants growing in the borders. He seemed completely oblivious of his pupil's quite obvious agitation. I noticed that my friend kept feeling his head and guessed that the laudanum was having its usual after-effect of producing a mild headache. Thank God, at least, that he was alive.

'We had no chance to exchange more than a brief morning greeting before the Marchese appeared. Knowing what was coming I almost exhaled a sigh of relief. Soon all would be over. I watched in horrid fascination as he donned, before my eyes, the mask of grief. Of course, knowing what I did, I was particularly sensitive to the changes in his countenance. All the same, his consummate skill as an actor repelled me. He made the announcement in a suitably grave voice, and we all stood staring at him, Lord Frederick as if turned to stone, Brookes making vague, distressed noises and myself silently containing my guilty knowledge.

'I held my breath, praying that Lord Frederick would say nothing. The Marchese concluded his announcement by saying, "In the circumstances, gentlemen, you will not take offence if I ask you to terminate your stay with us. It is the custom in Italy for relatives of a deceased person to enclose themselves away from the world for a period of forty days and nights."

'Lord Frederick was making small choking noises. I longed to run and comfort him, but did not do so for fear of revealing too much to the acutely discerning eye of the Marchese. "H ... how did she ...?" he managed at last.

' "With a dagger," replied that reptile of a man, sparing my friend nothing. "Straight through her heart."

'Looking back I think it was as well that the shock poor Lord Frederick sustained that morning practically deprived him of the powers of speech and motion. Brookes and I half carried him back into the house and up the stairs, and deposited him like a sack of potatoes in his chamber.

' "I think we should depart without taking breakfast," I told a totally bewildered Brookes. "We can find a *taverna* somewhere along the road."

'Brookes ruffled his sparse hair and looked down at his charge, who was now slumped in a chair and weeping quietly into his pocket handkerchief. "I cannot think," said he, "why Lord Frederick should be so greatly affected by the demise of the young lady. She is, when all is said and done, scarcely known to him. I confess to feeling much regret myself. Signorina di Ludovici was a very beautiful young lady, and I think it quite shocking that she should take her own life for some obscure reason. Lord Frederick is, of course, a peculiarly *sensitive* young man, despite his high spirits. Do you think we really should leave without taking refreshment? Would it not seem discourteous?"

'He rattled on, almost as upset in his own way as I was, but covering it all with a

148

superfluity of words. I managed to persuade him that to depart at once was the best course, and he was again bewildered when not a single member of the family, nor yet one of the servants, came to assist us with our luggage and to wish us God-speed. He kept muttering, "Most extraordinary!" as he bundled Lord Frederick's bags into the hired carriage, and then, "Quite untoward ... we must go on to Naples I suppose? ... I trust his lordship will have recovered by then..."

'As I sat in the carriage beside Lord Frederick, not casting a backward glance at the villa which had once looked so delightful to my English eyes, the picture which rose before me was not of Gabriella enduring the agony and solitude of a nun's cell, deprived of food and company, but of the Marchese and Marchesa breakfasting with Paolo and Katrina and making pleasant, cultivated conversation. I wondered if the sores on Gabriella's back would oulast those in her heart.'

SEPTEMBER, 1790

Amelia is Married

As in Italy, so in the village of Piddingfold, the course of true love was not running smoothly. Amelia's Lothario had persuaded William

Darker to put forward the date of his eldest daughter's nuptials with the observation that ' 'Tis considered in fashionable circles that six months is long enough to mourn a husband or wife, and that one will not be thought wanting in feeling if one puts aside the trappings at the end of this period.' Clarissa Darker having died in December, William compromised and announced a date in September for the wedding, having no desire to forfeit such a useful business connection as Sir Edward had lately turned out to be. The elderly baronet had ventured to try his hand as a maltster and was purchasing all the barley William could produce. This saved the latter a good deal of time spent in hard bargaining at the Corn Exchange in Lewes.

Amelia Darker, who had not been consulted on the matter of her future, now had just four weeks of freedom left to her, and had fallen into that dangerous state of resignation which boded little good in terms of happiness. It was not like Amelia to go down without a fight, but the absence of James was proving to be a more powerful factor in the case than she had realised. She had no one save herself to champion her cause, and she was too unselfish to expect her more timid sisters to badger William on her behalf.

Papa knew nothing about that other gentleman in her life. Even had she plucked up the courage to tell him he would have brushed the whole thing aside as mere infatuation pointing out, reasonably enough, that the daughter of a gentleman simply could not marry a tradesman, however honourable his intentions. Now if a man had made a fortune through trade that would be an entirely different matter. The daughters of earls had been known to stoop and pick up a millionaire brewer, for instance. Johnny Perkins of Barclay Perkins and Company could tell you a thing or two about that.

Meanwhile, Mr. Frost, making his frequent and fruitless trips to Frinton Park, laden with toilet-water for the young ladies and Frisby's Backache Pills for Cook, knew the bitter anguish of waning hope, and although he sometimes met with his beloved alone in the shop the sweetness had gone out of their trysting.

*   *   *

On an unusually hot afternoon in September, when the whole of Piddingfold village seemed to have dropped into slumber, and the only sound to be heard was the droning of bees in the mass of columbine which clung to the churchyard wall, the bell of Mr. Frost's establishment tinkled and the door opened wide to admit the portly figure of Sir Edward Mulliner. Mr. Frost, emerging from his mahogany box, saw with a start that the enemy

151

had invaded his territory.

Sir Edward was affable, if a trifle pompous. 'Young man, do you have any lavender-water? I wish to purchase one of those fancy red flagons tied up with ribbon.'

For her? Of course for her. There was no other lady in the life of this breathless old lover. With a sick sensation in his stomach Mr. Frost fetched down from the shelf a dainty red glass flagon, encased in a little wicker basket, and placed it on the counter. Sir Edward nodded his satisfaction and produced from the pocket of his waistcoat a large silver guinea case. As he extracted the gleaming gold coin he was reminded of yet another purchase he wished to make. 'A bottle of laudanum, if you please, Mr. Frost.'

The apothecary did his best to look solicitous. 'Your gout is paining you again, Sir Edward?'

Sir Edward grunted assent and made a face. 'M'leg swelled up like a pumpkin last night. Didn't get a wink of sleep, and then, to cap all, m'head started to ache. Can't do without m'sleep.'

'Would you like me to examine your leg?' offered Mr. Frost politely. He was nothing if not conscientious in the exercise of his profession. Even the despised ones merited his concern—medically speaking.

The other shook his head impatiently. 'Looking at it'll do precious little good, young man. *I* can *look* at the deuced thing. It ain't a pretty sight, and it don't make a ha'p'orth of difference.'

Unable to resist throwing a scare into this fat buffoon who had filched his beloved, Mr. Frost offered suggestively, 'I have a great deal of experience in these things, Sir Edward, and would know better than you whether the disease has yet reached a critical stage.'

Sir Edward frowned and snapped shut his guinea case. 'Don't take your meaning, sir.'

Mr. Frost suppressed an unworthy smile. 'Gout is a progressive disease, Sir Edward. If the swelling progresses upwards beyond the knee, there is always the possibility of an apoplexy occurring.'

The purple-red bloom on Sir Edward's cheek disappeared, to be replaced by a rather unpleasant greenish glow. 'D'ye mean I might take a fit?'

The apothecary nodded gravely and persisted with wicked eagerness, 'Does the swelling reach beyond the knee?'

Sir Edward glanced down at the offending limb, clad in its expensive fawn broadcloth and its equally expensive brown leather boot, which last his valet had reluctantly been forced to slit at the top in order to accommodate the swelling. 'Well, yes,' he admitted grudgingly, 'now you mention it, it does.'

Mr. Frost tried to inject a note of sympathy into his voice. 'Ah, yes, I see, most distressing.'

'Is there anything that can be done?' asked his customer a thought anxiously.

Mr. Frost was brisk now that his professional services had been officially called upon. 'Laudanum is certainly not the cure,' he said severely. 'It will serve to alleviate the pain, but it will not effect a cure, since it merely serves to mask the symptoms.

'Now my remedy for gout is three drops of hiera picra to be taken in water last thing at night. This will reduce the swelling and lessen the chances of your throwing a fit.'

Something in Mr. Frost's tone caused Sir Edward to glance at him sharply, but the young man's face was as sober as a judge's, so he concluded that he must have been mistaken in supposing that the apothecary was deriving a certain amount of deplorable enjoyment from another's pain. Mr. Frost was the last person to make mock of a sick man. Anyone could have told you that. 'I'll take some,' he said at once.

Mr. Frost smiled approval of this sensible decision and having wrapped the three articles in question gave change for the guinea. Sir Edward had his hand on the door, had actually opened it and was about to step outside to the sound of Mr. Frost's 'Goodday to you, Sir Edward!' when something seemed to stop him in his tracks. He hesitated, still with his hand on the door, and with his back to the apothecary, for at least fifteen seconds, then, having obviously reached a difficult decision, he gave a quick glance up and down the street, presumably to make sure that no one was approaching the shop with intent to purchase, and slamming the door shut returned in some agitation to the counter.

Mr. Frost looked surprised, as well he might, for Sir Edward's manner was furtive in the extreme. Leaning both elbows on the counter the gentleman crooked his finger at the apothecary and whispered hoarsely, 'I've a rash ... in m'groin. Some ointment I thought ... or something?'

The young man's face paled. 'A rash?' he repeated stupidly, and even as he said the word his ears started to buzz and a momentary dizziness took possession of him. With an effort he pulled himself together and managed to ask the right questions. 'Does the rash itch?' It did.

'Are there small pustules?' There were.

'How long has the rash been in evidence?' It was noticed a month ago.

Mr. Frost turned his back upon the loathsome face so close to his, so cosily conspiratorial that it sickened him afresh, and reached for the mercury pills. 'Three to be taken twice a day,' he prescribed in a voice filled with contempt. 'That will be another four shillings and sixpence, if you please.' No 'Sir Edward' this time, just the plain, insolently couched request for his money. Sir Edward handed it over and without another word fled the shop.

When he had gone, taking with him the strong aroma of 'Prince's' snuff, Robert Frost repaired to the back kitchen of his premises and vomited into the sink. Meticulously, and with legs which threatened to give way under him at any moment, he cleaned and disinfected the places he had soiled. Then he staggered to a chair and flopped into it, supporting his head with his hands. Amelia, his sweet-tempered, gentle, sensible Amelia, whom nature had treated so cruelly, was about to be subjected to yet more cruelty at the hands of a diseased brute of a husband who would surely infect her with his obscene curse.

*   *   *

Only two weeks now before she got into bed with that old man. She sat on the churchyard wall, looking down at the daisies which grew in a thick carpet on the grave of Patience Westlake. They reminded her of the crocheted spread which Aunt Georgiana had made for her bed. Patience's bedspread, fashioned for her by nature, was, Amelia thought, the more beautiful. I wonder what you looked like, Patience. Were you beautiful? Did men desire you? Were you really a murderess like they say?

A shadow fell across the mound and she glanced up to see Parson Ellsworthy, forty years old and too shy to be anything except a bachelor, standing smiling down at her. 'Miss Amelia, good-afternoon to you.' He coughed, searching for an opening gambit, an exercise at which he was singularly maladroit. 'Soon I shall be addressing you as Lady Mulliner. How very grand you will become, with your own servants and carriages.'

It was kindly meant. The sort of remark he would have made to her when she was a child, akin with 'Miss Amelia, I hear that you are soon to make your debút into society. How very grown-up you will look with your hair dressed in the newest fashion.'

Parson Ellsworthy had always been kind, kind and uncritical and ineffectual, dedicated to the conversion to goodness of his over-eating, hard-drinking, profane and fornicating flock. Amelia smiled bravely back, swallowed miserably and bent down to pick a daisy. This was done so that he should not see her quivering mouth and over-bright eyes. He was not, as she might have imagined, entirely oblivious to her feelings. He understood more than she gave him credit for. He had seen many brides, most of them young, innocent and in the first bloom of youth, standing mutely beside portly or withered bridegrooms, living sacrifices to the power of money. Most bore themselves proudly, putting to shame the parents who had forced them into submission; a few wept openly, sobbing through the responses and soaking the pages of his prayer-book on which reposed the nuptial ring. In his wilder flights of imagination Parson Ellsworthy had fancied that gold symbol of servitude being placed not upon the young lady's finger but through her nose, after which the bridegroom would lead his prize down the aisle on the end of a pole!

Amelia Darker would conduct herself properly. She was really quite beautiful, and that mark on her face seemed to have faded a little. Art or nature? He could not be sure. Sensing that she would find any discussion of her forthcoming marriage distasteful he looked down at the mound and said the first thing that came into his head. 'May the earth rest lightly upon her bones.'

Amelia fixed him with a look of grave intensity. 'Patience? You mean Patience, sir?'

His dark, bovine gaze shifted, and he replied with a measure of embarrassment, 'Mrs. Westlake, yes.'

'You know her history?'

'Something of it,' he replied cautiously.

'Tell me.'

His eyes met hers and she felt ashamed to have provoked such unease. 'I gave my word that I would never speak of it to you or to your brother and sisters.'

'You gave your word to Papa?'

'Yes.'

'Then of course I shall not press you, but I

should like to know one thing.'

'I will tell you if I can.'

'Was she a very bad woman?'

'No, oh no,' was his immediate response, and then, 'Some would say so, but I think that she followed the dictates of her heart instead of adopting the more sensible course which was to use her head.'

'Oh, I see,' she replied with quick perception. 'Hers was a crime of passion.'

He seemed startled. Miss Amelia was more intelligent than most young women of his acquaintance. 'I would much prefer not to pursue the matter.'

'Of course not.' She slipped off the wall. 'I must go home now. It is nearly time for tea and Sir Edward is expected.'

'How very pleasant.'

'Yes.'

She was gone, picking her way through the tombstones to the path, leaving him with the feeling that the connection which had existed between them since her childhood had at last been broken. Augusta met her sister at the garden door. 'Oh, Amelia, Papa asked me to look for you. Sir Edward sent his manservant over to say that his master is indisposed and cannot come for tea.'

'Good,' Amelia said brightly, 'that means I shall not have to defend my honour!'

*   *   *

Sir Edward Mulliner had now become a frequent visitor to the apothecary's establishment in the High Street, his gout having become distinctly less troublesome, and the rash in his groin a mere pink patch on the surface of his skin. This last was a tremendous relief to him in view of his forthcoming nuptials. There was, however, one other small thing troubling him which did not seem to be responding to treatment.

As he entered Mr. Frost's shop on yet another mild September day he was in time to greet Miss Charlotte Lambton, one of Mr. Henry Lambton's silly girls, emerging with a sealing-waxed package clutched tightly in her hand. Sir Edward raised his hat. 'Good-morning, Miss Charlotte. There are none indisposed at home I hope?'

Miss Charlotte, by way of reply, clapped a hand to her mouth to stifle her giggles and ran for dear life, leaving Sir Edward frowning after her. That young baggage was not the first to throw a fit of hysterics at sight of him lately. They all thought him too long in the tooth to be marrying again. He could imagine the gossip that was going on behind his back.

Mr. Frost, palms flat on the counter, was ready and waiting to serve him. Sir Edward gave him a curt greeting, ordered some more hiera picra for his gout, and relayed the information that the rash in his groin had quite gone. Mr. Frost nodded in apparent satisfaction and took down a bottle of hiera picra. 'That will be two shillings and elevenpence three-farthings, if you please, Sir Edward.'

Sir Edward grunted, made no move to extract his guinea case, and lowered his ponderous backside on to the high stool provided for customers. Mr. Frost could not help noticing with a little stab of envy the fine quality of his blue broadcloth frock-coat, which was decorated with silver buttons bearing his family crest and braided with black ribbed silk. The observant eye of the young apothecary travelled upwards to the falls of Ghent lace at his customer's throat, and the tall, wide-brimmed, very expensive beaver hat. He imagined Amelia dressed in the fine clothes Sir Edward would undoubtedly provide for her and his heart gave a little lurch.

Sir Edward had one hand pressed to his stomach, just at the point where the heavy gold chain of his beautiful Feure watch, with its wind-on family portraits, was spread across his blue and white striped waistcoat. 'Deuced flatulence,' he rumbled, 'can't get rid of it ... plagues me day and night with the devil of a pain. Feels like someone has a knife in m'guts and gives it a twist now and then.'

'The James's powder which I prescribed should have afforded you relief, Sir Edward.'

'It did,' agreed that afflicted gentleman, 'but only temporarily. The pain came back again

161

within an hour or two and was as bad as ever. A week ago I had to put off a visit to my future wife because I felt too nauseated to drive in the carriage.'

'Mmm.' Mr. Frost bit his lip pensively. 'You may, of course, be suffering from a pustule in the stomach. If that is the case, Sir Edward, you will have to be exceedingly careful about your diet. Nothing must enter your stomach which can irritate the lining in the least degree.'

Sir Edward received this intelligence in glum silence. He was a good trencherman, fond of his food and drink, and the thought of resorting to 'pap' was disagreeable in the extreme. If it was the only means to cure him, however ... 'I shall be guided by you, sir,' he said morosely. 'You seem to know what you are about. Cured m'gout and m'cl ... m'rash.'

Your clap, old man, is not cured, Mr. Frost silently cautioned. It has merely retreated for a while. It lurks like a hungry wild beast, deep in your vitals, waiting to spring out and devour your innocent bride. Competently, Mr. Frost measured out a quantity of James's powder, poured it into a twist and sealed the opening with red wax. 'Half a teaspoonful to be taken after meals three times a day,' he instructed.

'Same as before?' grumbled his patient. 'Do you not have anything else I can try?'

'Yes,' returned Mr. Frost crisply. 'Abstinence is extremely efficacious for your condition, sir. You might try that.'

162

Insolent young dog. Did he imagine that his sharp nose for an ailment gave him the right to speak his mind to his betters? Sir Edward longed to put his thought into words, but the pain in his belly forbade it. He needed the apothecary for the time being, but he'd make it his business to lure a decently qualified physician into the county as soon as may be. He was getting a thought bored at being treated by a quack. With the briefest possible nod of thanks Sir Edward paid for his purchases and left the shop. Sadly Mr. Frost reflected that it was now only two days before Amelia Darker would be lost to him for ever.

*   *   *

The young lady so much in Mr. Frost's mind, thoroughly depressed by the preparations for her wedding and the dressmaker's constant attendance at Frinton Park bearing lengths of palest green silk for the bridesmaids' dresses, and several different shades of violet velvet for the bride's travelling pelisses, departed one afternoon to visit her friend, Lottie Lambton, who lived with her family at Glynwood Manor. Only two days remained before she must step into her gilded prison to endure God knew what atrocities at the hands of her gaoler. Amelia's depression was increased by the lack of news from the Continent. James had not written for several weeks, and even Papa was becoming a trifle worried. Checks made with the Earl of Adur had produced only gloomy corroboration. That villain Fred had not written either and nor, what was worse, had Mr. Brookes, who should have had enough sense of responsibility and care for his position to keep his employer informed of the whereabouts of his son. The Earl was prepared to wait another month before he set his bloodhound, in the shape of his attorney-at-law, Mr. Braithwaite, on the trail of the travellers. Privately, Amelia thought that James and Lord Frederick were having too good a time to bother with letter-writing, but she did not make this opinion known to her father for fear it would put him out of temper.

She chose to walk the mile to Glynwood Manor, enjoying the warm September sunshine, and at the same time noting the sinister signs of approaching winter, the guelder rose berries, bright as rubies in the hedgerows, the Michaelmas daisies flourishing in the cottage borders, the leaves already beginning to change colour on the beech tree which grew in the front garden of Parson Ellsworthy's house. That gentleman, busy with fork and hoe, waved to her as she passed, giving her his usual courteous greeting. She thought how strange it was that people like Parson Ellsworthy and Mr. Frost were considered by the gentry as the lower orders of society, not fit to marry their daughters. Such men were so much more attractive as personalities than the young bucks of the county who hunted ferociously, drank to excess and drove their horses with a careless eye on the animals' expendability. The lower orders might not be fortunate in the possession of great wealth, reflected Amelia, but they have infinitely more to offer one of my disposition than the Sir Edward Mulliners of this world.

Amelia remembered a remark of her mother's to the effect that one day women would have a say in the choice of a husband, since men could not remain the dominant race for ever. There was bound to be a reversal of roles at some time in the future. Towards the end of her life Clarissa Darker had been thought by many to be a little eccentric. Amelia had always listened to her mother with an open mind, discounting none of what William called 'your Mama's preposterous notions,' but she had the sad feeling that dear Mama had been born a hundred years too soon. In the year 1890 who knew what might happen? Meanwhile, women must remain, if not content with, at least submissive to, the wishes of their menfolk.

As she rounded the sweep leading to the front entrance of the Manor Amelia observed a gig being led away by a stable-boy. There was no mistaking the ownership either of the gig, which was badly in need of a coat of paint, or of the rather sway-backed animal drawing it. Mr.

Frost was in the house. Was he delivering something, or had he been summoned to attend a sick person? Should she beat a hasty retreat? Amelia was poised for flight when the front door of the house flew open and Lottie came tumbling down the steps waving one arm in greeting. The other supported a wooden trug. Too late to go back now. As the two friends drew nearer together Amelia asked, 'Is anyone unwell? I saw Mr. Frost's gig.'

Lottie giggled. 'That horrid old thing. I wonder he is not ashamed to go out in it.'

The remark calmed Amelia's fears. Lottie's high spirits clearly indicated that nothing alarming had occurred amongst the members of her family. Miss Lottie Lambton, her curly brown hair flying in all directions, her rosy cheeks bursting with good health, strode along, dragging Amelia with her, in the direction of the kitchen garden. 'It is Mama,' Amelia was informed. 'I went down to the village this morning to get her some James's powder for her megrim. She took some after dinner and went up to her room to lie down. After about half an hour she began to feel sick and rang for Agnes. Agnes said she was as white as a sheet and complaining of a pain, so Papa sent for Mr. Frost.'

'Oh dear, I do hope it is nothing serious,' Amelia said, newly alarmed.

'Shouldn't think so,' returned Lottie cheerfully. 'Mama has what is termed a

166

delicate stomach. She is always throwing up.'

In the kitchen garden the two girls picked rosemary, thyme, marjoram and basil to replenish Cook's herb-jars and chattered idly about the wedding, a subject which, to Amelia's chagrin, could not be avoided now that the wedding-day was almost upon her.

'Papa has received an offer from Mr. James Crumpler for me,' Lottie confided, and waited with a half-smile on her face for Amelia's reaction.

It was swift and incredulous. 'That ship-owner from Newporth, do you mean? But Lottie, he is awful! They say he beats his servants, his dogs and his horses, and he must be at least fifty!'

Lottie's berry-brown eyes were gaily mocking. 'I knew I could rely upon you, Milly, to speak the truth. He is almost as bad as yours, ain't he?'

'Oh, Lottie, I am so sorry, truly I am!' Amelia placed some sprigs of thyme into the trug and kissed her friend's cheek. 'What a vain and selfish creature I am, to be caught up with my own troubles and never giving a thought to others who might be in the same boat. Shall you mind terribly?'

'Not as terribly as you, dear Milly,' came the shrewd reply. 'I am made of sterner stuff. I shall devote myself to charitable works, and in bed I shall shut my eyes and grit my teeth, and make believe that he is a handsome young

167

beau. At least my children should bring me joy.'

'You are so sensible,' sighed Amelia, 'that is what I must do, of course.'

'It will help you to forget Mr. Frost.'

Amelia gave a little gasp of surprise. 'How did you ...? Oh, heavens, Lottie, you have not *told* anyone?'

Lottie eyed her reproachfully. 'As if I would, Milly. You know me better than that I hope.'

'Is it so very apparent then?'

'Every time you speak of him, and you speak of him a great deal.'

'Thank you, Lottie, for telling me,' Amelia answered primly. 'I shall remember to keep a guard on my tongue in future.'

'It might be as well,' agreed her friend. 'Even Sir Edward is not blind.'

'No.' Amelia felt even more depressed than before.

Lottie picked up the trug and they walked over the lawns towards the kitchen door. 'My Aunt Sophie was sweet on your Papa once,' Amelia said, 'but Papa picked out Mr. Briggs-Watson for her, so nothing came of it.'

Lottie did not answer. Sophie Briggs-Watson was not one of her Papa's favourite subjects. He could often be heard referring to her as 'a mischief-making old harridan'. That did not sound like long-lost love tied up with blue ribbon!

The girls handed over their herbs and

168

walked round to the front of the house, intending to stroll over the lawns to the park. Mr. Frost was coming down the steps and Lottie called out, 'Mr. Frost! Pray, how is Mama?'

He turned, and Amelia saw with a slight shock how white and drawn he looked. Had her proposed marriage affected him that much? As he caught sight of Amelia the apothecary's face changed subtly and she saw something in his expression which made her blood run cold. Was it, could it be, dislike? Was it fear? Oh, God, she should never have encouraged him. She should have rebuked him for presumption rather than give him false hope.

In these few remaining weeks before her marriage she had seen very little of him, thinking it advisable to allow the last tenuous threads of their relationship to break gently. She had not realised how greatly she had wronged him. Characteristically Amelia took all the blame upon herself. She was the guilty party, he the innocent victim of circumstances.

Mr. Frost gave her an almost cursory greeting before turning his full attention upon Lottie. 'Mrs. Lambton has had a severe disturbance of the stomach which has now happily subsided. I have prescribed a soothing draught, and Mrs. Lambton's maid Agnes is coming with me now to fetch the mixture.'

As if on cue Agnes emerged from round the

side of the house and ran towards the gig, mounting unaided. It would have been beneath even Mr. Frost's dignity to have assisted a servant into a vehicle. The apothecary felt in the pocket of his frock-coat and produced the packet of James's powder which Lottie had purchased that morning. He said, 'I am taking this in order to exchange it for plain bismuth. The remedy is quite obviously too strong for Mrs. Lambton's stomach.'

'But she has been taking James's powder for years without causing herself any harm,' Lottie said with a puzzled air.

'Quite so.' Mr. Frost smiled tightly. 'And her stomach has finally rebelled. It is often the way with people who continually take the same medicine for a chronic ailment.

'Oh, I see.' Lottie smiled. 'How fortunate we are to have such a very able man as yourself, doctor, to look after us.'

He accepted the compliment with another thin smile and a lift of his hat. 'Your servant, Miss Lambton ... Miss Darker.'

Amelia stared after him. 'He seems upset about something.'

Lottie's boisterous laugh dispelled dark thoughts. 'That is probably occasioned by the shock of discovering Mama to be genuinely indisposed for once.'

*   *   *

As Parson Ellsworthy had foreseen, Amelia

170

Darker was perfectly composed on her wedding-day. She stood beside her ageing bridegroom, making the responses in her sweet, clear voice, looking like an obedient doll in white satin and lace. The bridegroom, on the other hand, fidgeted abominably and when required to speak, did so in a voice so muffled and indistinct that one might suppose he had partaken too liberally of the bottle before coming to church. As if to dispute this theory there arose in the mind of the parson the knowledge that Sir Edward in his cups was loud, extremely articulate and jovial. He was curiously low-spirited for a practised imbiber.

'Those whom God hath joined together, let no man put asunder . . .'

They walked down the aisle slowly, she with her slight limp, he staggering . . . yes, decided Parson Ellsworthy, definitely staggering . . . a somewhat pathetic sight. It was not right. And yet I shall go on doing it, he thought. I shall go on marrying these incompatible couples, because if I do not I shall lose my living and I cannot afford that.

Amelia, though puzzled by her husband's low spirits, privately admitted to a feeling of relief. There would be no rowdy or unseemly scenes after the wedding-breakfast. He might not even be able to . . . She chided herself for such thoughts. She must learn to live with her destiny, however frightful it might prove to be.

In the carriage on the short drive back to

Frinton Park Amelia stole a glance at her bridegroom. He was sitting staring straight in front of him with one hand spread across his stomach. Indigestion again she supposed. He had become a martyr to it lately. It had reduced him as a man and had made it possible for her to remain alone with him, secure in the knowledge that he would make no unwelcome advances. There was nothing so dampening to the ardour of a lover than a pain in the gut. She laid a hand on his arm. 'Are you not well, Edward?'

He tried to smile at her, but it was more of a grimace. 'My stomach,' he confessed, confirming her suspicions. 'I shall take one of Frost's powders when we get within doors. It will pass ... it will pass...'

'Should you like to lie down in the guest chamber for a while?'

He squeezed out another tortured smile. 'So anxious to get me into bed, my dear?'

Her innocent face under the lace and orange-blossom turned bright red. 'Sir, I ...' She withdrew her hand from his arm, disgusted by the quip, and for the first time that morning felt close to tears. She ventured no further remark, and when the carriage pulled up in the sweep of Frinton Park she descended without his aid and went into the house.

She had the almost overwhelming urge to run up to her room, but long training by her mother in the social graces came to her

172

assistance and moving to the exact centre of the hall she stood waiting to receive her guests. Sir Edward wheezed up the steps to join her, and the servants came running into the hall to make their curtseys to the new Lady Mulliner. Soon the guests were filling the hall and offering their congratulations. The ladies touched Amelia's hot cheek with their lips and passed on with a smile and a rustle of satin or silk, the gentlemen bowed over her hand, complimented her on her looks and passed on too, relieved that their rumbling stomachs were about to receive impatiently awaited sustenance.

It ended at last and Sir Edward offered her his arm. Together, bride and groom walked towards the Eating Room, already noisy with conversation. Sir Edward immediately began fumbling in his pocket for his packet of powder, which he intended to open as soon as he sat down. A second before his hand encountered the crisp white paper he fell like a stone to the floor.

The ladies shrieked and the gentlemen made startled, deep-throated noises as they bent over the prostrate figure. Water, brandy, rum and port were called for in turn and advice given to 'Loosen his stock!' 'Burn a feather under his nose!' 'Open his breeches!' this last countered with 'Do not, I pray, open his breeches before the ladies!' 'Open his waistcoat then. He must have air,' and all this while at least five and twenty personages, hovering over the fallen baronet made quite certain that he inhaled the minimum amount of air possible.

At length it was decided to remove Sir Edward to the upper regions of the house and William sent for the Head Footman, the Head Groom, the Under-gardener and two stable-boys to transport Sir Edward's not inconsiderable bulk to the guest-chamber. Once deposited on the four-poster the stricken man appeared to recover somewhat and apologised to his host in wheezy accents for his 'dashed foolishness'.

William brushed aside the apology and declared his intention of sending for Dr. Lyford from Lewes. There were certain occasions upon which young Mr. Frost, competent and helpful though he was, simply would not do. Qualified he might be to practise as an apothecary, but he still lacked the higher degree of physician and could not be expected to diagnose ailments of a more serious nature. Sir Edward had been complaining of pain and faintness for some weeks now. It was high time that he consulted a highly-qualified medical practitioner.

The patient protested but was out-voted, both by his wife and by his father-in-law, the latter at the same time deciding that the wedding-breakfast should proceed so as not to disappoint the company. William turned to his daughter, who stood mutely beside him looking down at the pain-racked figure on the bed. 'Go and change out of your finery, Amelia, and then come back to sit with your husband until the physician comes. You shall have a tray sent up.'

'Yes, Father.' Sadly Amelia repaired to her room, taking care to lock the door behind her. It was like a blow in the face to be reminded that this was no longer her own special and private domain, the discreet, unbetraying receptacle for all her hopes and fears. She flung herself full-length on the bed and wept. The sound of voices drifting up from the Eating Room below floated through the open casement. She thought she heard someone say, 'Poor Amelia.'

Luke Potter, one of the stable-boys, took Sir William's own stallion and covered the eight miles to Lewes in under an hour. He returned with the physician upon the stroke of four, riding in the latter's gig and leaving his master's horse to be fed and watered in the town's livery stables.

The merry-makers were now disporting themselves in the upstairs saloon, dancing to the music of horn, pipe and fiddle. Dr. Lyford caught sight of a host of whirling figures as he passed the open doors of the largest room in the house and proceeded to make his way to the guest-chamber, William in attendance.

Amelia, stiff and cramped after three hours of sitting with the invalid, rose as Dr. Lyford entered and came to greet him. He gave her a look half-sympathetic, half-inquiring. 'Lady Mulliner?'

It was the first time that anyone had addressed her by her new title and Amelia experienced an odd sensation of unreality. 'Oh ... yes,' she answered vaguely. Supposing her to be struck dumb by grief Dr. Lyford appealed to William. 'What seems to be the trouble, Mr. Darker?'

William said he really had very little idea, except that he knew his friend to be suffering from some disorder in the region of his stomach. He had been complaining of discomfort for several weeks now, and upon his arrival at Frinton Park in the morning had dropped like a sack of coals. Amelia, at last finding her voice, confirmed that her husband had recovered consciousness quite quickly and that the pain had now greatly diminished.

'Hmm.' Dr. Lyford busied himself with his black bag and requested a few moments alone with the patient in order to make his examination and diagnosis. Sir Edward, who, since the advent of the physician had been totally ignored, began testily grumbling about 'a lot of fuss over trifles.'

'As to that, we shall soon see,' replied Dr. Lyford briskly, and firmly ejected William and Amelia from the room. Like children they waited obediently outside the bedroom door, listening to the sounds of revelry coming from the saloon, both imbued with the strange feeling that they had nothing at all to do with the festivities going on in the house. For the first time William began to regret having given his consent to this unequal union. As always with such regrets it came too late. He took his daughter's hand in his and she, with her quick intuitiveness divined his thoughts. 'I am sure that it is nothing serious, Papa.'

They waited about ten minutes before the door opened and Dr. Lyford emerged. He was frowning, and Amelia's heart gave a funny little lurch. Of hope or fear? William came straight to the point. 'Is he seriously ill?'

The physician's keen blue eyes registered irritation. 'Overdosed,' he snapped. 'Taking this and that for every ailment under the sun, real or imaginary. Who has been treating him?'

William looked a little sheepish. 'In these parts we all go to young Mr. Frost the apothecary,' he confessed. He added charitably, 'He is very well thought of.'

'May be, may be.' Dr. Lyford pursed his lips and shook his head dismissingly, unwilling to admit that an apothecary was qualified to prescribe anything more controversial than a purge or a headache powder. Originally members of the Grocers' Company, essentially tradesmen who prepared and administered the potions prescribed by the physicians, in recent years the apothecaries had begun to attend patients and prescribe drugs themselves. They were now functioning like physicians, treating ordinary and even serious cases and calling in the physician only when a second opinion was required.

It had all started with the Great Plague, of course, back in 1665 when the physicians, with cowardly haste, had fled to the country, leaving the apothecaries in undisputed possession of the field.

'These fellows have their uses,' he allowed grudgingly, 'but they are inclined to over-prescribe. Their livelihoods are made out of and depend upon the selling of drugs, d'ye see? The money they get from consultations is not enough to keep a dog alive.' Dr. Lyford extracted a pocket handkerchief from the sleeve of his coat and blew his nose in short, staccato blasts before continuing, 'Sir Edward tells me that he has been taking hiera picra for gout, juniper seeds for headaches, James's powders for indigestion and ...' —a quick glance at Amelia pulled him up short. Nearly let the cat out of the bag there—'and ...' hastily he improvised, 'er, various other things for minor indispositions. I have given him very strict instructions that he must take nothing except the medicine I shall prescribe, which is a diuretic designed to clear the blood of poisons and to purify the system. I am not in favour of bleeding at the moment as he is a little weak from the pain he has endured.'

He looked rather hard at Amelia. 'I am very much afraid, Lady Mulliner, that your wedding tour will have to be put off for a while. Sir Edward is in no condition to travel.'

'We were not intending to travel until we make our Christmas visits,' Amelia said dully.

'No, quite so.' Dr. Lyford's unspoken comment was that elderly gentlemen should not make a habit of gadding about in carriages for pleasure.

After a few minutes of further conversation the physician took his leave, promising to call at Sir Edward's home at Firlcumbe Hall the next day to examine his patient, and expressing the hope that he would find him greatly restored. He remembered to wish the bride good fortune.

When Amelia looked in on her husband he was on his feet and endeavouring to straighten his crumpled frock-coat. A healthier colour had returned to his face.

'Are you feeling better, sir?'

His large grin embraced her. 'Come here, wife!'

She stared at him. The grin widened, turned lecherous. 'You must not play the timid virgin with me now.'

'I ... sir, I ...' Amelia picked up her skirts with the intention of taking flight, but he was too quick for her. She let out a little scream as he grabbed her from behind, but he knocked the breath clean out of her by pitching her on to the bed and throwing himself on top of her.

A frantic, undignified tearing at garments

ensued while Amelia, quite forgetting that she was now Sir Edward's wife and that her honour was safe, struggled to wriggle out from underneath the mound of flesh and bone which was pinning her to the bed. She was brought to a realisation of her changed condition by Sir Edward's high-pitched insistence, 'You are my wife ... my wife ... my wife!' while all the time his hands clawed at her bodice, ripping it apart like an eager child unwrapping a Christmas package. Three minutes sufficed to render her as naked as the day she was born and all she could do was to lie there like a cornered rabbit while Sir Edward hastily divested himself of his clothes, panting heavily as he struggled with buttons and laces. The sight of that slowly emerging, shapeless heap of white flesh and a brief glimpse of purplish-red genitals made Amelia feel faint. She hoped desperately that she would faint and that whatever was about to take place would proceed without her knowledge. She remembered Lottie Lambton's words, 'I shall close my eyes and grit my teeth and hope to have joy of my children,' or something like that. Amelia closed her eyes and gritted her teeth and gave a little moan of fright as his mouth came down on hers and his tongue forced its way between her teeth.

Other, more terrifying things began to happen, things for which Clarissa had not prepared her daughter, and she began to struggle again, because surely there should not be so much pain attached to the coupling of a man and a woman.

Amelia wrenched her mouth free from the imprisoning wetness and took a deep breath. Her hands pushed at the flabby chest adhering stickily to her breasts, but she had not the strength to move it more than a quarter of an inch. 'No, please no ... oh, please do not.'

She began to weep, but the pain continued, got worse and then abruptly eased as he withdrew himself and rolled away from her. Oh, God, it was worse, much worse than she had anticipated. Was it going to be like this all the time? How often would he demand that she undergo this humiliating ritual? Was she now carrying his seed? Could a child actually be born of this terrible, wicked act? Amelia became conscious that she was making the most awful animal noises. She controlled herself with an effort and lay listening to the strains of a quadrille coming from the saloon. They were out there celebrating the fact that she had just been raped by a disgusting old man.

Resolutely, Amelia took herself to task. She *must not think like that*. She must behave with dignity, whatever the unpleasantness she was forced to undergo. She must begin by getting up, here and now, and donning her torn gown. With luck she might be able to get to her bedroom without being seen and change it for another. Then she must go and mingle with her guests as though nothing in the world was wrong.

Amelia sat up and sneaked a glance at her husband. He was lying flat on his back with his eyes and mouth wide open. The eyes had a fixed glare the like of which she had only seen once before in her life. Her grandfather, Sir Charles Branson, had looked like that when they had brought him back on a shutter after a fall from his horse. Grandfather Branson had been dead before they could get him back to the house.

NOVEMBER, 1790

Letter from James Darker to his father, William Darker

'Dear Papa,

'I hope you received my letter from Naples describing Lord Frederick's slight indisposition. The physician in Naples said it was the heat that was the cause of the fever which overcame Lord Frederick. He was bled for three days running. The treatment proved very effective, and within a week the patient was on his feet again and able to come with Mr. Brookes and myself to see the famous bay.

'Naples overflows with life. It is full of little brown children jumping about stark naked. There is a certain breed there called the Lazzaroni, which means the poor and diseased. Once a day they take off their dirty rags and bathe in the sea. They are expert pickpockets and haunt the inns and taverns. We witnessed one very strange and barbarous ceremony. It took place on the nineteenth day of September, which is the anniversary of the death of St. Gennaro. On that day a phial of the saint's blood is taken from the cathedral and made to liquefy. I saw it with my own eyes, a dirty brown dust in a glass container which suddenly changed to a bright red liquid as the Cardinal held it up for the people to see. Of course, it was a trick, but a very clever one, for neither Lord Frederick nor myself could see how it was done. We were told that last year the Cardinal was unable to make the blood liquefy for a whole hour, while the people stood round him yelling abuse at their saint for refusing to oblige!

'While we were in Naples we went to the theatre and were treated to the sight of the King and Queen of the two Sicilies. He is Ferdinand I, son of the Habsburg Charles III of Spain. She is an Austrian princess, plain and inelegant, like the wife of a tradesman.

'We could not leave Italy without visiting

Mount Vesuvius and made the ascent on horse-back. Mr. Brookes, whom I have come greatly to admire for his earnest attention to the smallest detail, went to the very top of the crater and came back with his clothes alight in half a dozen places! We had him doused in very short order, you may be sure.

'Having travelled northwards, making sure to visit towns we had not passed on the way down, we are now in the German Empire. The roads are appalling here and it is not possible to travel more than fifteen miles a day. We are now reduced to staying at inns, and shall be so until we reach Vienna, where we are to take lodgings for a month or six weeks.

'I thought the inns in Italy were bad enough. Here one must sleep in a common chamber with all sorts and conditions of low fellows who bring in their dogs to lie down beside them, chaining them to the bed. Greasy black sausage with sauerkraut, a kind of vinegary cabbage, seems to be the staple diet here. We stopped at Carlsbad to take the waters, which are said to be good for barren women. They contain chalk, red bolus, nitre-allem vitrol, iron and sulphur. They taste quite foul.

'Mr. Brookes was all for making the rounds of the petty German courts, of which there are no less than sixty, but we managed to dissuade him from this because of the ceremony involved in obtaining access to "regal presences" as Lord Frederick calls them. Invariably too, one is expected to present gifts, which can make the whole thing rather hard on one's pocket. It really is not worth the bother. Mr. Brookes was disappointed at not seeing the 'royals' at the court of Hanover in view of their connection with our own Royal Family, but Lord Frederick assured him that all Germans look alike, an answer which he condemned as "most unsatisfactory."

'We are at present on our way to Vienna and hope to get there by the middle of December. As far as I know we shall remain there for about a month and then cross the border into the Low Countries. This will be the last stage of our journey, and I expect we shall be home in time to enjoy the onset of spring.

'I received your letter dated the eighth of July soon after I left Rome, and am not a little surprised that you should have given your consent to Amelia marrying Sir Edward Mulliner. I hope that nothing is settled yet, and should very much like to know Amelia's feelings on the subject. She is very dear to me, and I should not like to think that she was being coerced into marriage. Forgive me, Papa, if I sound critical, but I shall be of age in a week or two and have a right to express an opinion concerning the future of my sisters. I know you will respect that right.

'Give my best love to everyone at home and I hope that Aunt Sophie has not got half the foxes in the county terrified out of their wits.'

'Your affectionate son, James Darker.'

'Dated this twenty-seventh day
of November, 1790.'

*   *   *

Letter from Amelia, Lady Mulliner to her brother, James Darker.

'My dearest James,
'I am addressing this letter *Poste Restante*, Vienna in the hope that you will have arrived there by the time it has winged its way across the Channel and travelled overland. You will have heard from Papa I think that I am to be married to Sir Edward Mulliner. Since Papa wrote that letter the marriage has taken place and I am already a widow. Sir Edward died on the very day of the ceremony from a pustule in the stomach. Dear James, this must come as a terrible shock to you, but I always think that bad news is best delivered quickly, without beating about the bush. Now do not be

angry or get yourself into the mood to tilt at windmills on my behalf. I freely admit that when Papa told me of the match he had negotiated for me I was frankly horrified, and remained so till my wedding day. I shed many tears in the privacy of my chamber and asked God to please send home my dearest brother James, who would do his best to extricate me from the snare Papa had set for me.

'Apart from a natural repugnance to marry a man three times my age, and a grandfather to boot, I now confess that I was in love with another. Mr. Frost the apothecary had engaged my affections, and together we decided to fight Papa with all the weapons in our armoury. What were those weapons? You may well ask, for in the end they proved to be as ephemeral as the breeze.

'Mr. Frost was no knight errant and I no Lady Mary Wortley Montague. Our love died for lack of nourishment, and while he contented himself with languishing glances whenever we met, I gradually drifted into a state of resignation, and even began to see one or two advantages to be gained from marrying Sir Edward. I saw these advantages and used them to convince myself that marriage to an old man would not be so horrible as my fancy dictated.

'On the very day of our union my bridegroom was taken ill and Papa sent to

Lewes for Dr. Lyford. The patient was pronounced not to be in a dangerous condition. A minor irritation of the stomach lining was the diagnosis. Rest, medicine and regular monthly bleeding were prescribed, all of which recommendations I intended to follow to the letter. My concern for the invalid proved of no avail, however. He died at about five o'clock on the day of our wedding and was buried in the churchyard of St. Nicholas at Brighthelmstone, where his first wife is laid to rest.

'Papa and the girls were very much upset. For my part, I could not pretend to a grief I did not feel and would not 'put on a show' for the benefit of the community. I am now the mistress of Firlcumbe Hall, Sir Edward having willed the property to me before our marriage. The estate is not entailed, and therefore his eldest son has no claim upon it.

'The Mulliners came to the wedding *en bloc*, sons, daughters, grandsons, granddaughters, even two great-grandsons, and stared at me as if I were the original fallen woman. It was obvious that they regarded me as a scheming female who had caught the fancy of an old dotard. Can you imagine anything further from the truth? In fine, they were determined to dislike me, and though they kissed my cheek while offering their congratulations, the kiss meant nothing beyond a token of their willingness to preserve the conventions.

'Now that my husband is no more I do not intend to return to Frinton Park. Dear James, I know that *you* will understand. I am become my own mistress, with a house and servants of my own, and a substantial income with which to support all my grandeur. The eldest Mulliner says he will contest the will. Much good may it do him. Mr. Braithwaite informs me that any will drawn up by him is as water-tight as a barrel of smuggled Geneva, *and* that Charles Mulliner may litigate until he is blue in the face. He'll not shift the new Lady Mulliner.

'I so look forward to your return, James, but you will not find the same Amelia that you left behind. That should not trouble you, for I know you will think I have changed for the better. Remember that a welcome always awaits you at the house of "Amelia, Lady Mulliner."

'Dated this twelfth day of October, 1790.'

DECEMBER, 1790

Vienna

It was cold in Vienna, that gay, luxurious city which was to become ever gayer and ever more luxurious three decades from now. Christmas was approaching, and the River Danube was already frozen. Over the snow-covered ground the ladies took their recreation in fantastically shaped sledges painted in bright colours. Griffins, tigers, swans, scallop shells and dolphins swept along in the wake of trotting horses, bearing their precious and beautiful burdens, who preened themselves in their fur-lined velvets, displayed their laces and jewels, and inclined their velvet-capped heads at friends and acquaintances. The horses too were richly adorned, their glossy coats and flying manes set off with plumes of feathers, ribbons and bells. At night footmen rode before the sledges with lighted torches.

The two young men threw themselves with almost frenetic energy into the entertainments offered by this enchanting city, not least among which were the first-class riding and fencing schools. At the famous Imperial Spanish Riding School, built by the Empress Maria Theresa of Austria, they watched fascinated as high-born ladies and gentlemen rode round and round, schooling their horses in the laws of equitation, a science as yet in its infancy on the English scene.

On the surface Lord Frederick had recovered from his truly horrifying experience in Rome, although there were times when James sensed in his friend a reserve and a detachment which had not been there before.

Fred never spoke of the events which had taken place, and once, when James had ventured to suggest that 'It had all been for the best', his friend had directed at him a gentle, half-sorrowful smile accompanied by the request, 'Dear fellow, be good enough never to mention the subject again'.

James had felt snubbed, and Fred, immediately perceiving the hurt he had occasioned, put an arm about the other's shoulder in a silent gesture of love. The gesture seemed to say, 'We have shared great joys and great sadness together. Let us always retain the respect we now have for each other'.

One day, about a week before Christmas, James and Fred found themselves, as if by mutual consent, directing their footsteps towards the Spanish Riding School, leaving Mr. Brookes to explore the marvels of the Belvedere Palace. There was a gallery running all the way round the ring in which spectators could walk and admire the horses, or more particularly the *equestriennes* in their uniformly elegant riding habits of red velvet frogged with gold, and their little black tricorne hats, under which gleaming coils of hair were neatly netted.

These proud fillies, well aware of the impression they were making, walked, trotted, or cantered round the ring, backs ramrod straight, pretty heads aloof, appearing totally absorbed in their exercises, but sharply observing nonetheless every handsome gentleman who presumed to stare. Heaven help the gentleman who did not. His reputation would be in shreds before the evening!

'I bet I could get Cæsar to do that,' Fred said thoughtfully, pointing to a beautiful grey who was performing one of the complicated equitation exercises. 'I can train that stallion to do almost anything.'

'Mmm.' James watched fascinated as the grey changed step, lifting his front legs with the precision of a trained soldier. 'The trouble is, one needs to be trained oneself before one can pass it on to the horse.'

'There is a book on it,' Fred replied eagerly. 'It is printed in German, of course, but I think I can make it out. I shall purchase a copy and take it home with me.'

James laughed. 'My imagination pictures you training Cæsar on Piddingfold Green, with the reins in one hand and the book in the other. All the villagers will come and stare, decide after a minute or two that foreign travel has addled your brains, and send for his lordship to carry you off home.'

But Fred was not listening. His gaze was concentrated upon a woman who was being assisted to mount a fidgeting Lipizzaner. He turned startled eyes upon his friend. 'That woman over there. Of whom does she remind you?'

James obediently followed the direction of Fred's discreetly pointing finger. The woman had her face turned towards him, facing the Lipizzaner's rump as she mounted. James caught his breath. 'The Queen of France!'

In halting German Fred addressed a gentleman standing beside him. 'Sir, can you tell me the name of the lady who has just mounted the Lipizzaner?'

The man gave him an interested smile. 'That is the Emperor Leopold's sister, *Mein Herr*, the Princess Maria Amalia.'

'Of course!' Fred gave a little laugh. 'My friend and I have lately been in Paris, where we had the honour of speaking to the Queen of France, the lady's sister. They are very alike.'

The gentleman was even more interested, and posed a few casual questions before bowing and moving away. The two stayed on, held in thrall by the horses, unable to tear themselves away from the spectacle of perfect unison, horses and riders moving as one. Round and round they went, inducing an almost trance-like state in the watchers.

'Gentlemen, I hear that you have had an audience with my sister.' Her voice was low and musical, unlike that of her sister, Marie Antoinette, who spoke with a high-pitched fretfulness which was painful to listen to, and was not entirely due to her present wretched situation. James had not thought about it much at the time, but the difference was striking. The floor of the gallery being scarcely more than eighteen inches higher than that of the ring she was able to look down upon them from her lofty perch, aweing them by her regality and by the immaculateness of her attire. Instead of the regulation red and gold costume she wore black velvet; ornamented with silver lace and large silver buttons. Her small black cap sported a white ostrich feather. The whip in her hand was an extension of her gracefully poised arm.

The two young Englishmen bowed and promptly lost the use of their tongues. Her smile was slyly mocking. The Duchess of Parma was used to the effect she produced on the opposite sex. 'Was the Queen of France in good health and spirits?'

Fred swallowed and managed, 'In tolerably good spirits, Your Highness, considering the dangerous circumstances now prevailing in France.'

'Ah, yes. Poor Maria Antonia. She will need all the courage at her command during the coming months. Our brother Leopold may be Holy Roman Emperor, but his power does not reach into France. He can only fight with words those who seek to dethrone our sister.' The doll face, smooth as porcelain, showed little anxiety, and both young men received the same impression. Her Royal Highness, the Princess Maria Amalia of Parma's interest in her sister's plight was purely academic. Her words held an underlying element of spite which Fred at least was quick to detect. Her red lips parted to display perfectly white teeth. 'Gentlemen, you may be surprised to learn that your identity is known to me. My sister wrote to me of two gentlemen who had passed through Paris in May of this year and to whom a certain letter had been confided. Her Majesty's letter to me was necessarily vague since she can never be sure of her correspondence remaining a secret between herself and the recipient, but from the way she described you both I think there can be no doubt.' An embarrassed Fred found himself on the end of a piercing blue stare. 'Not very many people have been endowed by nature with that particular shade of hair. It is so very *outré*!' The laugh that accompanied these last words was rather boisterous.

Fred continued to look embarrassed, bowed again and introduced himself, after which James was presented. A tiny inclination of the head acknowledged the introductions, while the superb Lipizzaner disdained even to look in the direction of the strangers and pawed the ground impatiently. 'I am relieved to know,' said Fred, 'that Her Majesty does manage to get some of her correspondence out of France. We were under the impression that the case was otherwise.'

The Princess smiled. 'It is difficult, of course, and sometimes the most extraordinary emissaries must be employed.' These last words were accompanied by a telling look at James, a look which caused him to fidget uneasily and lower his eyes. 'The letter is still in your possession, Lord Frederick?'

James waited with bated breath for his friend to reply, but Fred did not bat an eyelid as he lied, 'Certainly it is, Your Highness. I shall guard it with my life until I return to England.'

'You have not sent it on then?' The blue eyes were sharply inquisitive.

'I thought it more prudent not to do so, Your Highness. It might have fallen into the wrong hands.'

'Quite so.' She was silent for so long after this, pinioning them with that unwavering, oddly disconcerting regard, that they began to wonder whether they had been dismissed and had stupidly failed to pick up the signal. Fred, who objected to being treated as though he was a valued exhibit in a museum, was about to bow and retire when she asked, 'Are you staying in Vienna long?' For another week or two she was informed. 'And how do young English gentlemen amuse themselves during the evenings?' Concerts, perhaps, or the theatre? Would they care to come to the theatre tonight and share a box with her? They would? Well then, there was a performance of Shakespeare's 'Hamlet' at the Vienna State Theatre commencing at eight o'clock. Her carriage would come and collect them from their lodgings. Where were their lodgings? Ah, the Schuler Strasse. Yes, she knew it well. Her coachman would come for them at half-past seven o'clock. With a flick of her whip she sent the Lipizzaner trotting forward leaving behind her two rather overwhelmed young persons.

'Phew!' James fingered the lace at his neck, which he imagined was threatening to choke him. 'She made me feel like a country clodhopper.'

'She did little for my sense of superiority,' Fred admitted ruefully. 'Shall we watch her go round once or twice?'

James nodded eager agreement. 'I would not miss such a spectacle for the world.'

Her horsemanship was all that might be expected from one who had had a passion for horses from the age of three, and she regaled the admiring spectators with a performance which produced an unending stream of oohs and aahs and a shower of '*Wunderschöns!*' Her equitation exercises completed to her satisfaction she commenced a series of *cabriole* movements which changed the murmurs to gasps as the animal's front legs pawed the air and it seemed as if she must surely take a fall.

As they left the Riding School James quipped, 'Try that on Piddingfold Green and see where it gets you!'

Fred grinned. 'Over the top and straight into the duckpond I shouldn't wonder.'

The Vienna State Theatre was the city's most famous playhouse. The great Garrick had performed here, along with a host of other well-known actors and actresses from every country in Europe. The building's elegant façade of marble and gold seemed more in keeping with a royal palace than with a place of entertainment, but members of the Royal Family, a pride of Habsburgs, so often enjoyed themselves beneath its domed roof that the design of the building was not so incongruous as might at first be supposed.

Mr. Brookes, deeply impressed by this invitation from royalty which had been extended to his charges, had made sure that the young gentlemen were well turned out, even going to the length of running out to purchase a new pair of wrist-bands for Mr. Darker, whose old ones were disgracefully crumpled, and a set of gold buttons engraved with coronets for Lord Frederick. Showing great resource the tutor sewed the buttons on to Fred's frock-coat with his own hands.

The carriage arrived precisely at the time appointed and the short drive to the theatre was accomplished in ten minutes. Alighting from the vehicle, which moved off at a smart pace, Fred and James mingled with the crowds going in, slowly climbing the wide bank of steps leading to the colonnaded portico and passing into the carpeted foyer. The Viennese patrons had come out in their finest attire to grace the occasion and James was grateful that his best frock-coat and breeches had been tailored in London. Mr. Albert Penfold of Lewes was all very well, but he had not the expertise and flair of Mr. Jacob Moss and his assistants in Savile Row.

A liveried flunkey, approached by Fred, had difficulty in understanding that Lord Frederick Oliver and Mr. James Darker were expected in Her Royal Highness's box, but at last he found his way through the maze of Fred's stilted German and personally conducted them up a curving flight of stairs to the first floor of the theatre. He stopped before a door bearing the emblazoned arms of the House of Habsburg, ushered the young men inside and bade them be seated on chairs situated at the rear of the box. Her Royal Highness not yet having arrived they might wait here. They would please to remember to *stand* immediately Her Royal Highness put in an appearance.

'Does he think we have no manners?' complained Fred when the man had gone.

'He probably has a poor opinion of foreigners in general,' said James.

Fred pulled his mock-severe face. 'We are not foreigners, dear fellow. We are *English.*'

The stalls were filling with people and James was tempted to move to the front of the box to look down. Just in time Fred pulled him back. 'Not done, dear fellow,' he explained. 'They'll cheer anything that pops up in the royal box. Make you feel a dashed fool, what?'

The Princess arrived exactly five minutes before the performance was due to begin, accompanied by her husband, the Archduke Ferdinand of Parma, a tall, thin man with a large wart on the side of his nose, who accorded Fred the briefest of nods and totally ignored James, whom he did not consider fit company for Habsburgs and Bourbons. James, whose mind had been considerably broadened by travel, was impervious to such slights and cheerfully exchanged a wink with Fred.

In evening dress the Princess looked even more like her sister, though her expression was less strained. She wore blue satin banded with silver ribbon at waist and hem, and with three tiers of Alençon lace decorating her sleeves and décolletage. The Order of Maria Theresa sparkled over her left breast, a sunburst of diamonds enclosing an enamelled miniature of the Emperor Leopold II. Her blonde hair was covered by a wig powdered with diamonds and sapphires. Diamond and pearl-drop earrings completed her ensemble. She was forty-three and looked twenty-five.

She moved to the front of the box with her husband, acknowledging a rising murmur which might have been enthusiastic but sounded dutiful. As she sat down she beckoned Fred to her and indicated the chair on her left-hand side. A vague gesture of the hand directed at James suggested that he might sit anywhere he pleased provided it was behind her. James, nothing loth to melt into obscurity, sat as far back as possible and made up his mind to enjoy the performance. His pleasure was somewhat dimmed by the fact that the whole piece was spoken in German, but he knew the English version almost by heart and managed to follow the play pretty well.

At the conclusion of the performance the Princess did not invite her two guests to supper as Fred had suggested she might, and they went back to their lodgings feeling rather flat. As Fred remarked, 'Half the fun of going to the theatre is eating out afterwards. The company is invariably lively and there is a chance or two to make a conquest.'

James sneaked a sidelong glance at his friend as they strode through the lighted streets—Vienna was the first town in the Empire to be lit by gas—and tried to guess the other's state of mind. Had he so soon forgotten Gabriella? Fred, with his usual devilish intuition, caught James in his mind-reading act and said casually, 'Dear fellow, a man has to satisfy his bodily appetites. It don't *mean* anything, and anyway that affair in Rome has begun to take on all the aspects of a vivid dream. I sometimes wonder if it really happened. I put it down to the constant change of scene we have been experiencing.' He laughed awkwardly.

'Travel—the panacea for bereavement.'

It'll come up and hit you later James thought grimly. Aloud he said, without much enthusiasm, 'We could find a bawdy-house.'

Fred yawned. 'Not for me. The Princess has quite put me off women for the time being. She seems to have that wretched letter on her mind. She kept asking me if Louis had written it with his own hand, and was it sealed? Which last, of course, was an oblique way of asking me if I had read it. They can be dashed insulting, these royals, when they give their minds to it. She made me feel mighty uncomfortable, especially since the deuced letter was burned at least six months ago.'

'Should you not have told her the truth?' James wanted to know.

'What!' Fred exploded into laughter. 'Dear fellow, can you imagine confessing to having destroyed a letter written by a *king*! For all I know I might be guilty of high treason. They still flay people alive for that in the Empire.'

James looked startled. Was Fred to be taken seriously? 'You have not done anything so terrible, have you, Fred?'

'Not so long as it don't go beyond us two, dear fellow.'

'No one shall hear anything from me,' James maintained stoutly.

A carriage came rushing at them down the Schuler Strasse, and they pressed themselves against the railings of a house. The occupants, two or three gentlemen with their 'ladies', waved as they went by and a flagon, presumably empty, whizzed past James's head.

'The people of Vienna have a wonderful capacity for enjoyment,' laughed Fred.

The front door of the house they had rented for their stay stood slightly ajar. Fred gave a quick frown. 'That is not like Brookes. What is the fellow thinking of? Anyone could get in.'

They came upon Arthur Brookes sprawled full-length on the floor of the saloon emitting a rhythmic series of groans which appeared to have been going on for some time. After according him a single startled glance they man-handled him to a chair. Fred, the ever-resourceful, burned a feather under his nose until he showed signs of reviving. Then the two young men turned their attention to the chaos surrounding them. The whole apartment was in disarray. Chairs and tables had been overturned, curtains pulled from their rods, pictures knocked askew and mirrors sent crashing to the floor.

As they moved about, setting things to rights and calling Mr. Brookes all kinds of an idiot for allowing access to intruders, pieces of broken china cracked under their feet. The miserable man in question sat nursing his head and was quite unable to give a coherent account of what had happened. 'Two of them I think,' he moaned ... 'blow to the back of the head ... did not get a chance to see ... took me completely by surprise. No, sir!' in answer to Fred's sharp query, 'I did not leave the door unlocked!'

They left him to mutter to himself and went to see what was missing. Ten minutes sufficed to assure them that all their possessions were intact. It looked like sheer vandalism. They remembered the roisterers in the carriage. 'Mohawks!' guessed Fred, 'a brand of Viennese Mohawks who rough up innocent citizens just for the fun of it.'

Satisfied with this explanation they assisted the bewildered Mr. Brookes to bed, and after taking a glass of brandy apiece repaired to their respective rooms for the night.

James was so tired after the day's sight-seeing, the evening's entertainment, and the assault upon the lodgings, that he fell back on the bed fully dressed and closed his eyes. He drifted into a light doze and would no doubt have sunk to a deeper level of unconsciousness for the remainder of the night had not rough hands been laid upon him. He did not stand a chance. Struggling up from sleep he tried to fight off a nightmare that was no nightmare at all but harsh, painful reality. There was to be no sweet relief in this awakening.

They had him trussed up like a chicken with his head swathed in a breath-stopping bag of some coarse material, and he had not even had time to cry out before his mouth was blocked with a cruel wooden gag secured in place by a wicked metal spring which clamped his teeth together. He made noises in his throat in protest against this violent outrage against his person and then desisted because he felt as if he was choking. He was being carried along now, and soon, sensing a coolness against the skin of his hands, he realised that he was out of doors. A rough manœuvring of his body told him that he was being bundled into a carriage.

The vehicle moved off and he sat propped between his two abductors, his mouth on fire from the barbarous gag, his face running with sweat under the stifling bag. On either side of him a hand gripped his arm above the elbow. He had not yet had time to feel fear or to ponder at length the reasons for this amazing act of abduction. He tried to gauge how far they were taking him by counting off the seconds, and had got to two hundred when pain, discomfort and the sinister beginnings of terror made him give up.

It seemed an eternity before the carriage rumbled to a stop. He was half-pushed, half-dragged out. His arms were once more enclosed in an iron grip and he was marched forward over cobblestones. The squeaking open of an iron gate, its clanging shut, 'Steps down', growled a voice in his ear. It was not an English voice. One, two, three, four ... twelve, and a horrid jarring of his spine as he took a thirteenth which was not there. Forward again, squeak, clang, 'Steps down', thirty-six in three sequences of twelve, walk, cold, damp and the unpleasant, unmistakable smell of mould penetrating the covering on his head.

Stop, sit down, the hardness of wood under his bottom and his arms tightly pinioned behind him, the coarse fibres of rope scratching his wrists, fingers at his neck, the sack removed from his head, the gag wrenched from his mouth, his eyes blinking in the light of wall torches. Wall torches? He was in an underground chamber, stone-walled and devoid of furniture. There were metal instruments on the walls, hanging from nails, objects which defied description. He had worked with farm implements all his life but had never seen anything remotely resembling those jagged-toothed hinged circles and long, pointed spikes, and that obscene metal case shaped like the human form.

Suddenly he became aware that a man was standing before him, short, stocky and anonymous in black, his face shadowed by a black, wide-brimmed hat. James stared up at him, attempting defiance to hide the terror mounting in his breast. 'What is the meaning of this? What right have you to carry me off and bring me here?' He felt something sliding down the sides of his mouth and guessed he had been wounded by the gag. Whoever had taken him prisoner was using rough methods.

The Englishness of the answering voice surprised him. There was only the merest trace of an accent in the soft, slightly husky tones. 'Mr. Darker, I will not, as you say in England, beat about the bush. You have been brought here rather than your friend, Lord Frederick Oliver, because you do not spring from the highest rank of the English aristocracy. As a member of the *lower* order of gentry it is felt that you will be more easily open to persuasion than your nobleman friend. In short, Mr. Darker, we wish to know the whereabouts of a certain letter which Lord Frederick Oliver received at the hands of His Majesty, King Louis of France.'

Light began to dawn. James said wonderingly, 'Our apartments. It was you! You were searching for the King's letter!'

The man retreated a step or two. 'And did not find it, Mr. Darker. Now, if you will please to tell me the whereabouts of that letter you are free to go.'

'Lord Frederick sent it on to London,' James replied at once.

This answer was met by a lingering silence, broken only by the drip drip of water coming from somewhere behind James's head. 'I think not, Mr. Darker,' the individual in black said at length. 'If that particular letter had reached London the repercussions would have been such that the whole of Europe would have resounded with them. Mr. Darker, I believe you do not know what is in that letter?'

'Indeed not. The letter was sealed.'

'Naturally. It is, as they say, inflammatory in content, and that is why those who employ me are anxious to ensure that it never does reach its destination.'

Inflammatory. The very same word that Fred had used. The man was pacing up and down now, with his fingers linked behind his back. 'You will be doing your country the greatest possible service, Mr. Darker, if you will but permit those in authority here to take possession of the letter.'

James made up his mind very quickly. Since the letter was no longer in existence there really was little point in playing complicated games with this personage, who so clearly had it in mind to add force to persuasion if gentle methods would not produce the desired result. 'The letter is destroyed,' he said emphatically, and he hoped convincingly. 'Lord Frederick thought it unwise to meddle in politics.'

'You are really very *stupid*, Mr. Darker,' and now the rasping voice was pitched a little higher, denoting the beginnings of anger. 'Do you expect me to believe that an English aristocrat would destroy a letter entrusted to his care by a *king*?'

'But it is true!' James strained at the bonds which secured him to the chair. 'I swear to you, sir, that the letter is no more. I saw it burned with my own eyes.'

The figure retreated a little further, merging with the shadows which lurked all round that

208

grim chamber. One hand was raised as if giving a signal, and in a trice James found himself flanked by two men, most probably those who had brought him hence. They each bent down and removed one of his boots. His stockings came off with the boots and he was left staring down at his naked, unprotected feet.

One of the men moved away and returned in a moment with a large pair of pincers which he had taken down from the wall. James flinched as these were brandished under his nose. Out of the shadows once more came his interrogator to stand before him, the blunt features just barely discernible beneath the concealing hat. He bent down, hands on his knees, looking like a father about to address a very young child. 'Mr. Darker, where is the letter?'

James shook his head dumbly, aware that his fright was pinned to his face like a badge, aware too that he was one of the lower order of gentry and could therefore be expected to show fear, aware that Fred would have smiled his gentle smile at this evil stranger and allowed him to do his worst while he spat in his face.

A flick of the man's fingers and now James's left foot was seized by one man while the other clamped the pincers round the big toe-nail and with a twist of his wrist wrenched it loose. Even as he screamed James looked down at the blood welling up all over his toe, his shocked mind refusing to believe that what was happening to him was not taking place in the midst of black nightmare. His second nightmare that evening. A pause of perhaps a minute before the relentless posing of that same unanswerable question, always prefaced politely by his name. 'Mr. Darker, where is the letter?'

'Burned, oh God, please believe me, it is burned, it is burned ... aaaaaaaaah!' and there was the second bloody little morsel caught fast in the grip of the pincers.

It went on until all ten of his toe-nails lay scattered at his feet and he sat with his head lolling over his breast and his mind fast disappearing into the black whirlpool of insensibility. He had fainted twice while they savaged his body, and twice they had revived him with water from a large earthenware pitcher. He came to as they were bundling him into a carriage, but was in too much pain, his brain too confused, to wonder where they were taking him. Had he been more alert he would have noticed that the journey was of approximately the same length as the previous one. At its conclusion he was brutally ejected from the carriage. He was unconscious again as he hit the roadway.

*   *   *

He recovered consciousness in his lodgings to find himself stretched full-length on the sofa with Fred and Mr. Brookes sitting beside him and, judging by the identical expressions on their faces, almost willing him to wake up. Immediately he became aware of the pain in his feet and looked along the length of his own body to observe two huge bandaged appendages on the end of his legs. An involuntary groan was dragged from him. 'My feet are on fire.'

'Dear fellow,' Fred patted his hand, 'are you well enough to tell us what happened?'

Painfully James ran through the events of the past three hours, concluding with the thought uppermost in his mind, the thought which would not be driven out by the torment he had suffered. 'They took me instead of you, Fred, because I do not belong to the upper rank of gentry and was therefore liable to break down under torture.'

His eyes, dark-rimmed from fatigue and the horrific experience he had been forced to undergo, searched Fred's face for signs of contempt as he confessed, 'I did break, Fred. I told him the letter was burned . . . but he did not believe me . . . so . . .'

The hand laid upon his tightened into a fist. 'Dear fellow, I should have done exactly the same in your place. There is no sense in being heroic over a non-existent letter. Now if I still had the letter and wanted very much to deliver it, that would be different, would it not? They might tear us to pieces and we should not say a word. Is not that so?'

'Yes.'

Mr. Brookes was scratching his head in bewilderment at all these references to a mysterious letter and cryptic hints of torture. He said, 'Gentlemen, forgive me if I seem lacking in intelligence, but I really am at a loss to know what all this is about. Mr. Darker is abducted and physically mutilated, *tortured* did you say? and all because he will not reveal the whereabouts of a certain letter. What letter, gentlemen?'

Briefly, Fred explained, and swore the tutor to secrecy. Mr. Brookes lapsed into unhappy silence. Conducting young gentlemen through Europe could turn out to be an alarming experience. 'We must get ourselves into the Low Countries as soon as may be,' decided Fred. 'I very much fear, Brookes, that we shall be unable to include the city of Prague in our itinerary. It belongs to the German Empire, and we are not safe until we are beyond the clutches of secret agents or spies, or whatever other nomenclature these people go by. If they have the audacity to lay violent hands upon an Englishman once they may yet try again ... with me as their victim next time.'

Mr. Brookes looked visibly shaken, though whether by the thought of his charge's possible abduction or by the disruption of his beloved itinerary was open to doubt. 'Do you think we should leave Vienna this week?'

'First thing tomorrow morning, my dear sir,'

replied Fred, the glint of determination in his eyes brooking no argument. 'You will please to help me pack up our luggage, then we can be off at dawn.'

Mr. Brookes bowed to the inevitable, rose from his chair, and departed for his bedroom in order to get together his effects. Fred turned his attention to James. 'I shall help you out of your clothes, dear fellow, pop you into bed and give you a drop or two of laudanum to make sure that you sleep for what is left of the night.' He consulted his pocket watch. 'By jingo, it is gone three o'clock!'

'Fred,' James's voice was low and urgent. 'I have been a coward ... no, let me go on,' as Fred started to expostulate. 'I should not have told that creature that the letter was burned. I should have stuck to my story that it had been sent on to London.'

'Nonsense!' Fred spread wide his hands. 'You say the fellow did not believe you, so what is the difference? You have given nothing away, and you have done the King of France a great service by all accounts.'

James struggled out of his blood-stained frock-coat. 'How?'

Fred leaned over to help him and then began to unbutton his friend's breeches. 'You tell me that your captor spoke of repercussions when the letter reached its destination?'

'Yes.'

'Well then, it looks to me as though Louis

213

had written something very very indiscreet in that accursed letter, something which his equally indiscreet spouse conveyed again by letter to her sister, our dear hostess of the evening, the Princess Maria Amalia who, by the way, you may blame for your present painful condition.'

'You think she is working against her sister then?'

'It would seem so. The French ship is sinking, dear fellow, and the rats are falling all over themselves to leave it. It appears to me that you and I, James, are the only two persons in this whole sordid affair who have acted sensibly. I, by burning the letter in the first place, and you by telling the Princess's minions that I had done so.'

After this James felt considerably more at ease in his mind. The worst thing in the world to him now would be to lose Fred's good opinion of him. 'I shall have to cut your breeches off, old fellow,' Fred said apologetically. 'It would be too painful the other way.'

He muttered under his breath as he fetched the scissors. 'Barbarians, bloody Habsburg barbarians. They have not emerged from the Dark Ages, from the time when they rampaged across Europe, raping and looting and generally creating mayhem.'

James lay back, white-faced and shivering now from the shock he had sustained. Fred was very much afraid that his friend would show signs of a fever by the morning, but there was no help for it, he must be got into a carriage and transported over the border into the Low Countries in the shortest time possible.

James was murmuring, half to himself, 'Why did they not kill me?'

Fred gave a last tug to his shirt. 'They thought they had, dear fellow. They left you right in the middle of the carriage-way. If the gentleman in the neighbouring house had not chanced to come along when he did you would have been a gonner.'

January, 1791

Amelia is Coerced

Sick at heart, Amelia stared at the haggard face of the apothecary. They were sitting in the withdrawing-room at Firlcumbe Hall, all white and gold stucco-work and bright yellow upholstered furniture. With the sunlight streaming in through the tall, round-headed windows, putting its Midas touch on the rich, dark sheen of mahogany and walnut the room had a warm, cheerful appearance belied only by the misery on the faces of its occupants. An unlikely setting for a confession to murder.

'I did it for you, Amelia,' he insisted. 'He was

riddled with the 'pox and it was not to be borne that he should infect you with his foul disease.'

'Poison,' she whispered. 'You *poisoned* him.'

He picked at his fingernails. 'That was not the intention, I do assure you. I meant only to make him too ill to ...' He broke off to stare at her miserably. 'I am not an evil man, Amelia, and I am not practised in the ways of the wrongdoer. I am so inept that I gave Miss Lambton one of the packets of powder I had intended for Sir Edward. She gave it to her mother and you know the result ... fortunately not fatal.'

'Oh, God!' She covered her face with her hands, looking small and defenceless in her black mourning gown, rocking backwards and forwards like a child. 'Why do you tell me this now? It is too cruel of you.'

'Amelia, please. Do you not see? I did it for *you*, so that you might be protected from that wretched, immoral creature. He was diseased, Amelia, and he would have passed his disease on to you, that dreadful scourge which he got from consorting with whores!'

She looked up, her eyes fiercely accusing. 'You can sit there and tell me that you committed a murder on my behalf? Did it never occur to you that I would rather have become infected with the 'pox than have the death of a man upon my conscience? Are you trying to pass the burden of your guilt on to me in order to ease your own black soul?'

'I cannot bear it alone.'

'What if I say *I will not share it with you*?'

He stared across the room at her, and the gentle brown eyes she had known were cold with the anguish of self-recrimination. 'You *must*, Amelia. If you do not I shall make known what I have done, and inevitably your part in it will come out.'

She rose from the chair in some agitation and moved over to one of the windows overlooking the park and the rolling downs beyond, surely one of the most beautiful views in all England. With her back to him she said, 'I do not understand you. Once I loved you and would have married you had not fate dictated otherwise. I thought you loved me.'

'I did. I *do*!' He was as distraught as she, desperately seeking to make her understand that he was not trying to put upon her some intolerable pressure, that his motive in coming to her was to make her see that only with her at his side could he learn to live with himself and outgrow the terrible harvest of guilt. The only other course was to do away with himself, and that his Puritan soul would not allow. He had it all worked out. When the period of mourning was over for her husband Amelia must marry him, become the staff he so badly needed to lean on. With her at his side he could go on living.

Her voice was quieter, more controlled. 'I presume you are making me a proposal of marriage?'

'Yes.'

'If you force me to accept it I shall hate you for the rest of my life.'

'I am prepared to take that chance.'

Her eyes followed the flight of a magpie which came to perch in the huge oak marking the limit of the park. 'One for sorrow, two for joy ...' and she knew that she was beaten. She could not, would not, give up all that she had gained, this house, the security of a large fortune, the independence to handle her own affairs. Ah, but, said a voice inside her. If you marry Mr. Frost all that you have will become his. And that would be better, said yet another voice, than coming under suspicion of murder. Then you would lose all.

The thought occurred to Amelia that this was not the first time that someone from Frinton Park had had to do with murder. Patience Westlake had been a murderess and hanged for it too. Amelia, Lady Mulliner, was an accessory, albeit unwittingly, to murder. She imagined the scandal that would result from any rash revelations made by Mr. Frost. How the tongues of Piddingfold and district would wag. Yes, she was trapped, and was it not a strange irony of fate that the man she had once wanted so much to marry should have become the man she least wanted to marry now?

She turned away from the window and

resumed her seat, placing her arms along the arms of her chair as though to steady herself. 'It would seem, Mr. Frost, that I have very little choice other than to marry you.'

He fell on his knees before her, abject as a chastised dog, his brown eyes begging for a token of affection. 'I shall become your devoted slave, Amelia. You will never regret your decision, I swear it.'

His eagerness repelled her, but she perceived one ray of light in this wretched situation. Mr. Frost's prickly conscience could become a very powerful weapon in her hands. It would enable her to remain mistress in her own house.

There was a great deal of her father in Amelia Mulliner and a little of her mother. Clarissa Darker had been of a kind and generous disposition. In the early days of her marriage she had been forced to come to terms with a situation which went quite against her natural instincts for fair play. It had not changed her for the worse, but it had bludgeoned into quiescence the rebellious elements in her character which prompted her to speak out against injustice and unfairness. So would it be with Amelia. Like Clarissa, she was about to settle for security.

JANUARY/FEBRUARY, 1791

A Strange Encounter

The threads of our lives are interwoven with those of others, they grow taut, break and are brought together again in the strangest possible circumstances. Dr. Robert Hollins looked down at the tossing figure of the young man stretched out on the bed and his mind went back twenty years to a cold December day in Lewes, Sussex, when a young physician called Robert Westlake had taken to wife one Patience Pochin, spinster of the parish of Piddingfold. The memory sickened him. He pushed it aside and turned to the thin, fair young man who had summoned the only English physician in Cleves, not knowing that the long arm of coincidence had reached out to meddle and play its mischievous little tricks. The name Oliver, given to him by the stout matron who brought the message, had meant nothing to Dr. Hollins, and he had arrived at the house in the Anna Straat expecting to find a patient of that name awaiting his services. Instead, he had looked down with complete disbelief at a blend of only too well-remembered lineaments, and even before Lord Frederick said, 'This is Mr. James Darker,' memories of Clarissa and William Darker had flooded his mind.

The patient was in no condition to be communicative, which enabled Dr. Hollins to recover his composure before proceeding with his examination. 'Perhaps,' he said, addressing Lord Frederick, 'you will be so kind, sir, as to inform me of the circumstances leading up to Mr. Darker's present condition?'

All the time he was speaking the physician's hands were busy with the clasps of his black bag, clicking them open, taking out various instruments and placing them in precise formation on a small table which stood beside the bed. Fred watched these manoeuvres almost with a sense of pleasure. They inspired confidence. But how to tell this grave fellow that his friend James had had all his toe-nails torn out, one by one, with the aid of pincers, by the agents of the Princess Maria Amalia of Parma, in order to make him reveal the whereabouts of a certain letter? Fred's ingenuity was stretched to the limit, and he came up with something barely plausible. 'Sir, it happened in Vienna. Some ruffians waylaid Mr. Darker on his way home from the theatre, demanded money which he had not got in his possession, and fell upon him when he could not produce it. They were all in a high state of intoxication and vented their rage at gaining nothing by removing Mr. Darker's toe-nails with pincers.'

Dr. Hollins looked suitably shocked—and

frankly incredulous. Immediately he turned his attention to James's feet, and having removed the bandage, drew in his breath sharply. 'How long ago did this happen?'

'Three weeks,' replied Fred impassively.

'Three weeks!' It was rarely if ever that Dr. Hollins raised his voice, but he came very close to it now. 'Whatever possessed you, sir, to travel over four hundred miles with a man in this condition? Great heavens, some of the finest physicians in the world live in Vienna.'

'Mr. Darker preferred to leave the Empire after being attacked, and he was not so ill when it first happened. At least he had no fever for the first ten days. He was, of course, in great pain.'

'That is quite obvious.' The physician's tone was now distinctly chilly. 'The toes are badly infected and Mr. Darker has a very high fever. You have not sent for me a moment too soon. Let us hope it is not too late.'

Fred went pale. 'You *can* help him, Dr. Hollins?'

'I shall do my best, naturally,' was all that was promised. The physician got to work with lancet and probe and took a perverse pleasure in commandeering Fred as his assistant. Fred bore it bravely, aided in his turn by Mr. Brookes, who, since the incident in Vienna had completely lost his taste for itineraries. James saved everyone a great deal of bother by fainting clean away.

222

Having bled the patient and left some pills to reduce his fever, and others to ease his pain, Dr. Hollins took his departure, promising to come again in the evening.

Fred thanked him profusely, and having seen him out, returned to sit by his friend. 'Dear fellow,' he said in a kind of weary desperation, 'you will greatly oblige me by getting well at once, before I really begin to think about your premature demise.'

*　　*　　*

It had been a nightmare journey from Vienna to Cleves, with eighteen changes of carriage and a fortune spent on bribes to rascally postilions and avaricious inn-keepers. James had become progressively worse, but Fred had not dared to stop sufficiently long to procure medical assistance for his friend until they were over the border. He wished now that he had taken a chance and stopped at Prague. Full of dreadful misgivings, Fred sat on beside James's restless figure, remembering the time at Frinton Park when he had declared with all the arrogance of eighteen years, 'We are going to have such fun on our Grand Tour!'

Twenty-four hours after Dr. Hollins's first visit James pulled out of his fever and complained of feeling hungry. 'Thank God!' exclaimed Mr. Brookes, a sentiment heartily endorsed by Fred.

Dr. Hollins watched his erstwhile patient eating with hearty appetite off his best Delftware and wondered whatever had possessed him to issue an invitation to supper to the son of a man who had once so deeply wronged him, and had bought his silence with £3,000. There was, of course, a twisted kind of pleasure in observing James Darker paying extravagant compliments to his charming, lively daughter, and in knowing that if the young man had any ideas in that direction they were never likely to come to fruition.

Reflected in the mirror which hung on the wall directly opposite his place at table Dr. Hollins saw a man of forty-five, prematurely aged by a life dedicated to the alleviation of suffering in others and a long pining for his native England. He had once been handsome, with a luxuriant growth of brown, curling hair, deep blue eyes and a wide, handsome smile, a smile which had once, long ago captured the heart of Miss Sophie Darker, she who had never forgiven him for his indifference towards her. He wondered what Sophie would think of him now, grey-haired and bent, with deeply-etched lines on his forehead.

He had been successful in his chosen profession, no one could deny that, and the beautiful French woman whom he had married three years after he left England, first for Amsterdam, afterwards settling in Cleves, had given him an equally beautiful daughter. It was not his wife's fault that he had never been able to eradicate his Englishness sufficiently to make her happy. She presided with remote graciousness over his household and knew as little about him as if he had been the Emperor of China. Mr. Darker was asking Claudine Hollins if she had ever visited England.

'No, sir, I hope that pleasure is still to come.' Her smile was enchanting, captivating. James thought he had never seen anything so beautiful as that smile and the way it made her blue eyes dance. Whenever he asked a question her face lit up, making him feel that he was the cleverest fellow alive, and that every word that fell from his lips was a positive pearl of wisdom.

'If ever you do come to England, Miss Hollins, you must visit us at our home in Piddingfold in Sussex,' James said enthusiastically. 'You will find the countryside quite different from that in the Low Countries.'

'Do I detect a hint of disparagement in your tone, Mr. Darker, when you speak of our Dutch landscape?' Dr. Hollins's smile was slightly strained.

James laughed. 'The pastures of home are very dear to me.'

'And to me,' put in Fred cheerfully. 'I shall not be sorry to gallop my stallion over Ditchley

Down in pursuit of Mr. Fox.'

James and Fred exchanged excited, almost conspiratorial glances. Home was very near and tugging more insistently as each day passed. Damn them, thought the physician as he sipped his claret. Damn their careless, youthful arrogance, and damn them for reminding me of what I have been so sorely missing for twenty years. He had, with exceeding difficulty, learned to live with his exile. These young men had committed the unforgivable sin of making him remember.

He looked at his wife and daughter, two elegantly attired, completely un-English females, who had little or no idea of the deep yearning he had for his native soil, or of the abiding hatred he nurtured for him who had been instrumental in ejecting him from it. Now these two youths and their tutor, who had plummeted down into his safe little world without any warning, had brought all the old feelings bubbling to the surface, had opened up all the old wounds which he had foolishly imagined had ceased to ache. Certainly the wounds had healed, but the scars remained.

The dining-room of his house, which he had always considered to be such a pleasant place to eat in, now seemed small, and a little too unpretentious, with its black and white chequered floor and solid oak dresser and table, perhaps because he was now mentally comparing it with that other, more splendid

Eating Room at Frinton Park, and the memories thus evoked were like silent stab wounds taking place inside him.

The talk was becoming more animated as Fred described in detail the hazards and joys of chasing a fox across twelve miles of downland, where it was possible to encounter totally unexpected obstacles. 'I remember once,' he reminisced, embracing everyone at table with his lively expression, 'Mr. Thornton, who is a farmer neighbour of ours, left a pile of turnips behind the hedge bordering his ten-acre field. Says he, the evening before the hunt is to meet, "You may ride through the ten-acre field tomorrow, gentlemen, for 'tis fallow this year and no harm done if you churn it up a bit." Well, needless to say, we took him at his word, and the next day there was I, with two others, head-first up to our fetlocks in turnips. Our mounts shied at the sight of these round white objects, d'ye see, and we were thrown. It left us in no gentle frame of mind I can tell you.'

It was the manner of telling rather than the actual tale which produced such lively and immediate response from the ladies, who laughed till the tears ran down their cheeks, and it was at that precise moment, when his two womenfolk seemed to fall completely under the spell of the gentlemen from Sussex, that the desire for revenge, which had lain so long dormant in the breast of Dr. Hollins, suddenly boiled up and came to a head, ejecting its invisible poisonous fumes to envelop the unsuspecting persons of the dinner-guests. Dr. Hollins had reached a spur-of-the-moment, but quite irreversible decision. If what he envisaged came to pass his revenge would be sweet indeed. The son of the man who had wronged him all those years ago should, if he wished, marry his daughter Claudine. His Claudine would become the progenitress of the next generation of Darkers.

Dr. Hollins was so amused by his own ingenuity that he choked on his apple pie and had to be slapped on the back while his wife administered a glass of water.

The physician's plan was not difficult to put into operation. Young James Darker, clearly infatuated, was never loth to accept an invitation to the modest house in the Prinsengracht, and although the travellers had declared their intention of sailing for England in time for the May-day junketings, in which they had a childish, but irresistible desire to participate, that was still six weeks away, long enough for an ardent wooer to declare himself.

Lord Frederick and Mr. Brookes were a problem, of course. They could never be excluded from an invitation. Fortunately their presence did not seem to inhibit James who, upon the flimsiest of pretexts, would entice Claudine into the garden 'to show me how the tulips are progressing,' or simply 'to admire the borders'.

Dr. Hollins would watch them walk off together with an indulgent smile, the glint of malice in his eyes observed only by his wife, who never thought to question its source. Desirée Hollins came from a family of devout French Huguenots, among whom the master's word was law. She would be sorry to lose her only daughter to the handsome young Englishman, but if Robert desired them to make a match of it there could be no gainsaying his will.

Things came to a head far more quickly than even Dr. Hollins had anticipated as he watched James daily becoming more and more enmeshed in the toils of love. Four weeks after the young men's arrival in Cleves Mr. James Darker requested an interview with Dr. Hollins, during the course of which he asked and was given permission to make a proposal of marriage to Claudine.

Fred, uneasily aware of what had been going on, but unwilling to poke his nose in where it was not wanted, begged leave to question his friend's decision to espouse himself to Mademoiselle Claudine, 'before a little matter awaiting your attention at home, dear fellow, has been satisfactorily resolved.'

'Miss Mary Houghton.'

'The same, dear fellow.'

'I have written to her,' James began slowly, wondering whether Fred would understand what he was about to say. 'I have told her that a marriage between us can only lead to wretchedness and unhappiness for both parties, and that she has my full permission to tell people that *she* has jilted *me*.'

'That will be a great comfort to her I am sure,' returned Fred drily.

The two were walking by the canal, idly pursuing the flight of a score of pintails which swooped down over the lime trees and came to rest on the glistening silver expanse of water. James, hands in his breeches pockets, stared thoughtfully down into the remarkably clean water of the canal and said with a new hardness in his voice, 'My mother married my father because she was made to, or rather because she felt obliged not to disappoint her parents. It is a pernicious thing, do you not think, Fred, when generation after generation of young people fetch up with partners chosen for them by old men and women who have forgotten what it is like to be young and in love, if they ever did know, and who haggle over money like Arabs in the market-place?'

Fred gave his light laugh. 'Dear fellow, I have always thought so, and in that I am more fortunate than you. As the son of a second marriage I am unimportant in the scheme of things and Papa will probably not frown upon any reasonably good marriage I may wish to make in the future.' He sighed briefly and James knew he was thinking of Gabriella. 'In your case,' he went on, 'as you are the eldest and indeed the only son, Frinton Park must come to you, and with it all the expenses that owning such a property incurs. In choosing Mary Houghton for you your father is showing himself to be a prudent business man, and ensuring that a large sum of capital will flow in to help maintain everyone in the manner to which they are accustomed. There are your sisters to be considered you know.'

James, who still knew nothing of Amelia's changed status, having left Vienna in a hurry on the exact day her letter reached the city, murmured agreement with Fred's sound and well-reasoned argument, but remained stubbornly determined to pursue the course he had mapped out for himself.

'Frinton Park means a very great deal to me,' he admitted, 'and as Claudine has no dowry it will mean that I shall have to work all the harder to maintain it.'

'It also means that if any of your sisters are still unmarried when your father dies, they will probably be forced to look lower down in the social scale because you have not the pecuniary means to raise them to the higher level.'

'And you think they will cry shame upon my head for not making better provision for them?'

Fred shrugged. 'Do not put words into my mouth, dear fellow. I am merely pointing out the pitfalls.'

'I have to marry where my heart dictates.'

'Now you begin to sound like Miss Fanny Burney.'

James burst out laughing. 'To speak truth, Fred, I am a thoroughly selfish fellow who is determined to have his own way, and what I have been asking you to do is to offer a sop to my conscience and tell me that I have every right to think of myself before I consider the interests of my family.'

'Precisely.'

'You know,' James said thoughtfully, 'I think we have learned far more than to appreciate a work of art on our Grand Tour.'

*   *   *

The wedding was a very quiet affair, Dr. Hollins and his wife having no relations on either side of the family living in Cleves. The physician had long since lost touch with his family in England, and as for Mrs. Hollins, she had outgrown, with a genteel shudder, the offshoots of the Paris *boulanger* from whose loins she had sprung.

There was to be no wedding tour until after the couple crossed the Channel to England, and even then, as James confessed, it might have to be postponed for a while. Papa would not take kindly to a second prolonged absence from home, especially since this one had produced such unexpected and not entirely agreeable—from William Darker's point of view—results.

'I am the happiest man alive,' James told his new father-in-law on the morning after his nuptials.

Dr. Hollins smiled understandingly. 'I am very glad, my dear sir. For myself, I could not wish for a more agreeable person than yourself to be my son-in-law. I trust that your father will not think you have acted too precipitately?'

'Papa is a very reserved man,' James replied cautiously, unwilling to reveal to the physician the extent of the muddle which awaited him at home. 'I expect he would have preferred me to marry a young lady well known to him, the daughter of one of his many friends, I suppose, but when he sees Claudine any doubts he may have will fly away with the wind. She is so very beautiful.' James's flushed face bore witness to his total infatuation. Only too well aware that enthusiasm for his newly-married status was running away with him, he tried to force his features into lines of sobriety, but they would keep melting into smiles.

'I very much regret the lack of dowry,' said the physician, watching him carefully.

'It is of no importance,' said James, and avoided the other's eye as he pronounced the lie.

The physician controlled a burst of laughter with difficulty. His memory of William Darker was of a man who regarded the acquisition of

233

money as of the utmost importance in the scheme of things. Twenty years could not have changed that particular aspect of his character. Aloud he said, 'Perhaps, James, you will take a letter from me to your father when you return to England? I should like to introduce myself and assure him that his new daughter-in-law comes from an entirely respectable family.'

'Of course, sir. I shall be delighted.'

'I understand that Claudine is taking you shopping this morning?'

'So I am informed. I am to give my opinion upon the newest fashions in ladies' headgear.'

'A very proper and absorbing occupation for a bridegroom,' approved Dr. Hollins. 'While you are gone I shall take the opportunity to pen the letter to your father. On second thoughts, I think I shall send it ahead of you, in order to lessen any slight shock which might be occasioned by your rather hasty marriage. We elderly gentlemen do not have the advantage of your youthful resilience.'

'That is very considerate of you, sir.'

'I believe that you are to sail on the eighteenth, provided the wind holds fair?'

'Yes, sir.'

Dr. Hollins produced an impressive sigh. 'I shall miss my daughter very much.'

'Oh, but surely, sir,' James said eagerly, 'we can expect a visit from you and Mrs. Hollins very soon?'

'We shall see.' And now the physician's

laughter simply could not be contained. It burst forth in a gigantic roar. James was not able to work out until much later just what it was he had said that was so excruciatingly funny.

*   *   *

Letter from Dr. Robert Hollins to Mr. William Darker of Frinton Park in Sussex—

'Dear Sir,
   'You will no doubt be astonished to hear from me after all these years, but by an extraordinary turn of fate, which none of us could ever have foreseen, our paths are destined to cross a second time.
   'It is twenty years now since you coerced me into accepting the blame for another, by means of threats and a bribe of £3,000. During all that time I have suffered the exquisite torture of the exile who knows that there is no return to the land where he has his roots, the invisible pull of which it has sometimes been almost impossible to resist. I held fast to my promise never to return, and have no intention of breaking it now, although that pledge, I fear, cannot be honoured by the next generation.
   'Allow me to explain. One night last January I was summoned to a house in the Anna Straat, which is not far from my own

235

home, by a young gentleman calling himself Lord Frederick Oliver. On arriving at the house in question I was introduced to a very sick young man whose features instantly struck a chord in my memory. When the name of the patient was revealed to me as James Darker I knew that this was none other than the son of William and Clarissa Darker whom I had known all those years ago in Sussex.

'Your son James was suffering from the effects, so Lord Frederick informed me, of an attack upon his person made by some ruffians in Vienna, who robbed him of his money and left him for dead. Let me put your mind at rest. The young man's strong constitution, combined with such treatment as I could give him, has fully restored him to health, and he is now in the best of spirits. Not wishing to bear a grudge for past injuries, I invited Mr. Darker, his friend, Lord Frederick, and their companion, Mr. Brookes, to dinner with myself, my wife and daughter, and a most enjoyable evening ensued.

'May I say here that I have at no time disclosed to your son my true identity, for I go by a different name here, thinking it prudent after I received news of the terrible occurrence in Piddingfold church and the subsequent doleful result. Here I am called Dr. Robert Hollins, and Mr. Darker and his friend continue to know me by that name.

'Our acquaintance was only of a fortnight's duration before I began to notice Mr. Darker paying marked attention to my daughter Claudine, which is not surprising since she is a very beautiful girl. I did nothing to deter him, for I saw no reason why the two should not make a match of it if fate so decreed.

'Imagine my pleasure when, just two months after they had first become acquainted, James asked my permission formally to propose to my daughter. I agreed, and a week later they were married, yesterday to be precise. I do pray most earnestly, sir, that you will agree with me that young people these days should be allowed to choose their marriage partners without regard to the pecuniary interests involved. From this you may gather that I was quite unable to offer Mr. Darker anything like a substantial dowry from his bride, but I do hope that you, sir, will accept the enclosed cheque for £4,800 which is no more than your due after twenty years. I have calculated the interest at three per cent per annum and trust you will think I have acted fairly towards you.

'I know you will agree with my sentiments when I say, may our children live in blessed harmony for many years, and may their children rejoice in the knowledge that their grand-parents were broad-minded enough to permit two people so very obviously in love to marry without let or hindrance. I look forward, sir, to the day when we two shall meet again and drink a glass of claret together in the saloon of Frinton Park, perhaps in a toast to our first grand-child.

'I remain, sir,

'Your obedient servant,

'Robert Hollins (Westlake).'

MARCH, 1791

The Homecoming

William Darker sat in the Morning Room of Frinton Park, his ears straining for the sound of carriage wheels, his mind greatly exercised in pondering the vagaries of fate, which had decreed that his only son should marry the daughter of a man he had not given more than a passing thought to for twenty years, a man he had wronged, a man who had waited a long, long time for his revenge.

As if that were not bad enough Amelia had announced her intention to marry Mr. Frost when her period of mourning for Sir Edward was over. Was ever a man so plagued by ill fortune? The thought popped into his head that this would never have happened if Clarissa had been alive. It would, of course. It was just that Clarissa had a way of soothing him down, of getting him to accept the inevitable without bursting a blood vessel. He missed her, by God he did, more now than when she had first been careless enough to lose her grip on life.

His daughters, including Amelia, who had come over from Firlcumbe Hall for the occasion, were chattering excitedly, the main item of speculation concerning the appearance of their new sister-in-law, whom they devoutly hoped would not out-do them in looks and deportment. William could hear references being made to her clothes, which, it seemed, were bound to be in the latest fashion 'because she is a foreigner.' The girls, knowing nothing of the bride's father and of his connection with the Darker family, remained in happy ignorance that they were irritating Papa almost beyond endurance with their incessant clack. As a distant low rumble sent them racing to the window William consoled himself with the thought that he had a big surprise in store for James, bigger by far than that young man could ever have imagined.

The next half-hour was taken up with over-effusive greetings, a stream of sentences begun and never finished because everybody spoke at once, and intermittent oohs and aahs going off like pistol shots. William allowed this excess of feminine enthusiasm to go on for a while before putting a stop to it by suggesting that

Amelia and her sisters should show Mrs. James Darker round the house.

James eyed his father apprehensively as his wife, completely enveloped by his sisters, disappeared. He would not, he decided, be the first to speak. He would allow William to dictate the tone of the interview, though he was curious to know why Amelia alone among his sisters was wearing black. Mama had been dead for over a year now.

William, having bowed his new daughter-in-law out of the Morning Room, resumed his seat and very deliberately went through the motions of lighting his pipe, an operation which took long enough to ensure that the returned traveller had been reduced to fidgeting with various china ornaments adorning the chiffonier. William's voice, coming from behind a positive battlefield of smoke, made James jump, 'Your Grand Tour was quite eventful.'

'Yes.'

'You must tell me about it over supper.'

'I shall be happy to do so, sir.'

'Miss Houghton received your letter, the one informing her that you intended to jilt her.'

James gave an exaggerated sigh at the heavy emphasis laid upon the word 'jilt.' 'I did not expect that you would understand, Father.'

William shot out his legs and contemplated the toes of his boots for a while before replying, 'I understand that you are a self-willed, insolent young dog who has no respect for his father.'

'Oh.' Another long drawn-out sigh. 'I see that we are to quarrel. I had hoped very much to avoid that.'

'Well, what in heaven's name did you *expect*?' William sounded exasperated rather than enraged, a fact which James duly noted and for which he was exceedingly thankful. 'Can you imagine,' William went on, 'how I felt when that Houghton woman showed me your letter?'

'If by "that Houghton woman" you mean *Mrs.* Houghton, may I remind you that the letter was not addressed to her!' This riposte was accompanied by a look of ferocious indignation which William swept aside with a wave of his hand. 'I suppose you expected the girl to keep it a secret from her Mama?'

'I thought ... I mean she always seemed a discreet sort of person ... she ...'

William interrupted his son's ramblings impatiently. 'What you thought, you scoundrel, was that Miss Houghton would be too ashamed to reveal the contents of your very cruel letter until circumstances forced her hand.'

'Let us not argue, Father,' James said wearily. 'What is done is done, and now two people who would have been disastrously mismatched stand a chance of attaining some happiness in life.'

William greeted this pious hope with a grunt and fell silent, puffing energetically on his pipe. Privately James was not a little astonished at his father's attitude towards his hurried marriage. He had expected verbal explosions and threats of eviction from Frinton Park, and he had even arranged with Fred to rent one of the houses on the Earl of Adur's estate, in the event of his finding himself homeless. Perhaps William was getting too old to fight.

William cut across his thoughts with a question. 'Your father-in-law is English I believe?'

James felt his body relax. The worst appeared to be over. 'Yes,' he answered brightly. 'He comes from Bagshot in Surrey, and chose to practise his profession in the Low Countries because he felt that medical science was more advanced there. He had no relations living in England when he moved to the Continent.'

'His wife is a Dutchwoman?'

'French. She is very beautiful.'

'And wealthy I suppose?' Robert Westlake was not one to choose a woman without a penny to her name.

James was looking surprised. 'I believe not. What a strange thing to say.'

William issued a warning to himself to be more careful. 'Not at all. Medical fellows always aim high. It is a well-known fact, which leads me on to inquire if you have heard from

Amelia.'

James frowned. 'No.'

'I thought she might have written to you.'

James hesitated. 'Er ... perhaps she did. We left Vienna just after I was attacked. I'll tell you more about that later. Did Amelia have something special to confide?'

William explained and was not surprised when James gave a careless shrug. A newly-married man, especially one who is foolish enough to fall in love with his wife, is not usually greatly concerned with the affairs of others. 'That is why I said medical fellows aim high.'

'Times are changing, Father.'

'For the worse it seems.'

James asked abruptly. 'What do you think of Claudine?'

William rose rather stiffly from the depths of his chair. Going over to the fireplace he knocked out his pipe. 'What do you want me to say? That she is beautiful? That she will make you a good wife? As to the first, I can say yes with perfect honesty. As to the second, only time will show. She is an unknown quantity, not even English.'

'You are angry because there is no dowry,' James accused.

'I was at first,' admitted his father.

'Does that mean that you are become reconciled to losing £150,000?'

'It is not lost.'

James gawped.

'*I* am going to marry Miss Mary Houghton. It is what your mother would have called a marriage of convenience.'

His son was aghast. 'Papa, how can you? Oh, heavens, Mary Houghton will be my stepmother! It is ... it is almost like incest ... I ...'

William was laughing at him. 'Boot's on the other foot now, is it not? *You* may run off and marry a dowerless fortune-hunter without asking my permission, but *I* may not marry a poor jilted female who cannot hold up her head in the county because my son has no sense of honour.'

'I told her she might say that *she* rejected *me*.'

'Pshaw!' William dismissed this airy-fairy notion with a noise of disgust. 'And who would believe her?'

'I shall have to leave Frinton Park.'

'That is up to you,' came the calm rejoinder. 'There will always be room for you, your wife and the children you may beget in my house. One day it will be your house, but do not forget that when I die Mary Houghton is entitled to live on here and enjoy the income from her widow's jointure. It will be your responsibility, James, to pay her £500 per annum for as long as she lives. I have made provision for that in my will ... and if she outlives you, your son will have to carry on with the annuity. You've paid a high price for your foolishness.'

James suddenly felt in need of fresh air. 'Excuse me, sir,' he said without warning. 'I am going for a walk. The carriage drive from Dover has made my head ache.'

William's mocking laughter followed him out into the hall and down the front steps into the sweep.

Almost by instinct James made his way to the churchyard. There he sat on the wall and looked down at the familiar headstone. A thrush alighted on the mound and began picking at a clump of groundsel. James followed its subsequent flight to a distant oak and tried to shake off the feeling of depression which had descended like a black cloud to accompany him all the way from the house. 'Patience,' he said, 'I have kept my promise to come and see you upon my return. Now you must tell me what I should do, for I do not know if I should stay in my father's house or not.'

He waited, confidently, and with the blind, unquestioning faith of his childhood, for her to answer.

We hope you have enjoyed this Large Print book. Other Chivers Press or G.K. Hall & Co. Large Print books are available at your library or directly from the publishers.

For more information about current and forthcoming titles, please call or write, without obligation, to:

Chivers Press Limited
Windsor Bridge Road
Bath BA2 3AX
England
Tel. (01225) 335336

OR

G.K. Hall & Co.
P.O. Box 159
Thorndike, Maine 04986
USA
Tel. (800) 223–2336

All our Large Print titles are designed for easy reading, and all our books are made to last.